"I need to hold y[...]

David's words pulled [...] had denied for so long [...] fragile control, she had to get them out of here. "Let's go up to the castle."

David grabbed her hand, and they ran across the piazza. Thunder rolled heavily across the sky, but he didn't say a word until they reached the hill. As she turned to him, the skies opened and the rain poured down.

She read the desire in his eyes as with strained movements, he pulled the wet blouse away from her breasts and watched the material mold itself to her.

"I want you," she admitted.

He crushed her to him and claimed her mouth. "Say you love me." His voice was hard with demand. "Say it!"

A lightning bolt hit the sea. "I love you!" she screamed as the thunder rolled over the water to envelop them in sound. "I love you," she whispered in the silence when the thunder stopped.

She loved him, but she could never have him. . . .

Hundreds of thousands of fans from around the world enjoy romance novels, and Harlequin is happy to have such an international fan club. One of the highlights of the year is the annual, glamorous Italian reader party—a thanks to our readers—and **Rita Clay Estrada** was the honored guest speaker last year. Rita had a fabulous time in Venice, but she didn't stop there. She toured Italy and spent several glorious days in Vernazza, the setting for her latest Temptation novel, *Twice Loved*. We hope you love it, too!

Cofounder and first president of Romance Writers of America, this talented author makes her home in Texas.

Books by Rita Clay Estrada

HARLEQUIN TEMPTATION
166–THE IVORY KEY
188–A LITTLE MAGIC
220–TRUST
265–SECOND TO NONE
313–TO BUY A GROOM
349–THE LADY SAYS NO

Twice Loved
RITA CLAY ESTRADA

Harlequin Books

TORONTO • NEW YORK • LONDON
AMSTERDAM • PARIS • SYDNEY • HAMBURG
STOCKHOLM • ATHENS • TOKYO • MILAN

To Skip Matthews,
for his friendship, laughter and no-nonsense advice.

To Linda and Frank Martinez,
for so many things, including fine wines at anniversaries,
oak trees and fun times.

To my brother, Greg Abrams,
who introduced me to Vernazza and then shared it with me.

And to my editor, Malle Vallik,
for all her well-done hard work, patience and good advice.

Thanks, all!

Published September 1991

ISBN 0-373-25461-X

TWICE LOVED

Prologue

Dear Diary,

This has got to be the most exciting thing that's ever happened to me! Imagine spending my last three weeks before college here, in Vernazza, Italy!

When my *beloved* cousin Tina fell in love with an Italian dream boat, I thought it was *trés* romantic. But I never *dreamed* she'd marry him and leave America! She actually came here to *live!* Bless her heart, but my cousin always seemed like such a feet-on-the-ground type of person. She may be only three years older than me, but sometimes she acts as though she was a hundred to my eighteen. Moving here is not something I would ever have imagined Tina Simpson, now Mrs. Arturo Sottosanti, doing. But if she had the nerve to change her name from simple to a mouthful, why not go all the way and live the avant-garde life in Europe? If I fell in love, which I won't, then I'd be expected to move to wherever my husband was. That's probably why I will *never* marry. It's just not the *feminist* thing to do.

Anyway, here's where my diary begins—in a fishing village called Vernazza on the rocky coastline south of the Italian Riviera. The area is called Cinque Terre, or Five Lands, because it has five points of land jutting into the Mediterranean with a medieval castle and village on each point. Isn't that just too neat?

So much for my first diary entry. I promised Mom that I'd keep this up for the duration of the trip. It'll be hard—I've never written my thoughts out before. But Mom says that years from now I'll look back and be able to relive my first impressions of Europe. She's had a diary since she was twelve, and she says she used it to remind her what that age was like when I got to be twelve and impossible. I'm willing to give it a try, but I think I'm a little old for this.

Dear Diary,

I slipped two cheese sandwiches and a bottle of water into my backpack and hiked to the next town. The well-worn path trailed across the tops of volcanic hills. All the way I had a stunning panorama of the Mediterranean, and at the top, the view of terraced vineyards. And castles on hills. This is fairy-tale country.

Maybe when I graduate, I'll find a job here and stay with Tina. We get along great, like we're sisters or something. Whenever I mention going home, I see a funny look in her eyes. Arturo must recognize it as homesickness, too, because he squeezes her hand or kisses her cheek. He knows she's going to miss me when I leave. But they're planning a trip to Louisiana on their first anniversary. They're *so* romantic. I think my mom and dad were like that. I wonder if I'll ever be that lucky.

Dear Diary,

I spent the most wonderful morning learning how to make, roll out and slice pasta dough. Tina had never made pasta, either, so her mother-in-law taught us. We looked like a takeoff of the "I Love Lucy" show. Tina is learning Italian and Mama Rosa is trying to learn English. I can pantomime really well. It sounds crazy, but we understood each other. By the time we all stopped our clumsy attempts to roll out the dough evenly, we were covered with flour from head to toe. I never laughed so hard!

I think this diary thing is growing on me. I might keep this up, but I'll call you a journal when I get home. After all, I'll be a freshman at Louisiana State.

Dear Diary,

I met the neatest guy today. His name is David Marshall, he's from Atlanta, Georgia and he just graduated from college. He's taking a break before he enters law school this fall. *Law school!* Imagine that! He's only four years older than I am. He's traveling with a friend, Jerry. I'm not too fond of Jerry. There's something about him that makes me nervous.

But I'm digressing, as Mom would say.

I was perched on my favorite rock right on the stone keep, writing a breezy, sophisticated postcard to Prom Queen Diedra so she'd die of envy, when I heard this deep voice ask me if it was my private rock. I started to say no but when I looked up, here was this *fantastic*-looking guy with a smile that turned me to mush. He's a little over six feet tall with dark hair. His eyes, when he took off his sunglasses, were a deep, penetrating blue. I couldn't think of a thing to say! I'm old enough to be in college. I'm old enough to be in Europe. I couldn't talk. The only word my mind hooked onto is one I couldn't say anyway. *Damn!*

He smiled again, then sat down beside me and stared out to sea. I stared at him. Up close, he was even more beautiful. And I still couldn't think of a single *witty* thing to say.

Now that I think about it, though, he didn't say much either. He just gave an occasional contented sigh. I'm not sure, but, I think he feels the same way about Cinque Terre that I do. After a long time, probably about an hour, we started reminiscing about home in the U. S. of A. and ourselves. When the sun tilted toward the horizon, we both stood at the same time and walked silently back to the church square. It was *so* romantic!

Dear Diary,

I saw David again today. We were both on the same hiking path heading for the next village. It's a three-hour walk, but the larger town has a beach of soft volcanic sand. Besides, with the amount of pasta I ate last night, I needed the walk.

Back to the main focus: David. We discussed records, movies, books and more records. We have so much in common! He laughs at my jokes and listens to my ideas as if I'm the wittiest or wisest woman in the world.

After we sunbathed on the beach, ate a slice of Italian pizza—which, Diary, is *nothing* like the American version—and walked back, most of the day was gone. As we rounded the last hill and looked down at the storybook village below, my gaze was caught by the narrow valley and the castle keep, rising darkly against the pale blue horizon, on the other side.

David stopped too. It was obvious that we both felt the same way. His hand came up and rested on my shoulder and his body heat traveled to deep inside me. I was afraid to breathe for fear he would move his hand away. For a single, splendid moment I felt a part of the earth, of the air, of Italy. It was wonderful and fragile. But what scared me the most was that I felt a part of David.

That's a thought I'm not ready to explore.

Dear Diary,

I met David one week ago and can't remember what my life was like before him. We meet each morning at our rock and plan our day. No matter what we do—as long as we're together—we have a great time!

I still don't like David's friend, Jerry. He always looks at me and smirks as if he knows something I don't. I get the feeling he'd like to ruin what David and I have. I've asked David about him several times, but he just shrugs and says Jerry's like that. Then he changes the subject. I think he's tired of his friend's funny ways, too, because we stay away from him.

Tonight was a very special night. We strolled the narrow winding streets of the fishing village. I said hello to several of Mama Rosa's friends sitting on benches, watching their grandchildren play while they exchanged gossip. Actually, I think they were watching us. And I think they thought we were a nice-looking couple because they kept smiling and nodding and whispering to each other.

Then we climbed to our favorite place, behind the castle and in front of the small cemetery on the top of the hill. Hand in hand, we watched the setting sun shadow the valley. Just before darkness became complete, David leaned against the castle wall and pulled me toward him. I rested against him, and we watched the sea go from orange red to deep black. It was beautiful and sad.

And then David kissed me! *Really kissed me.* It was the most wonderful moment in my life. When I finally found the strength to open my eyes, he was smiling down at me. Without another word, he led me down the trail to the village and we had a Coke on the steps of Saint Margaret's church as if we kissed every night.

And he calls me Annie instead of Suzanne. He says Suzanne is a name for an old woman. I've never had a nickname before. I love it.

For the rest of the night, whenever I looked at him he smiled so sweetly I was toasty warm all over.

Dear Diary,

I haven't kept up with you like I promised to do when I began this trip. So much has happened. I've grown so much in the past two weeks, I feel like I'm someone else in Suzanne's body. Tina keeps looking at me funny and asking me if everything is okay. I keep telling her it is, but I can see the concern in her eyes. I'm trying not to talk about David too much so she'll relax around him, instead of playing substitute mama. It's not easy to do.

Tonight we're going to watch the sunset at the castle keep again. But this time, David is bringing a picnic dinner. And he warned Jerry to stay away. I can't wait.

Dear Diary,

Two evenings ago, David and I became lovers. Lovers—what a wonderful, delightful, consenting-adult-type word. Still, it doesn't say enough.

We were holding each other and watching the moon rise over the mountain, when I began caressing David and he was touching me. Suddenly everything inside me changed and I wanted more. I *knew* what was going to happen, but I didn't know how or what to do. Soon I didn't care. Wherever David led me I followed. And I was right. He was the most gentle, kind and thoughtful man in the whole wide world. His touch was tender and arousing. And when we came together, I thought I was at the gates of heaven. I was. I will never be the same again. Never. David changed my body and my life.

I love him. I've known that for a week, but I was afraid to say—or write—anything because I thought we might never see each other again, and I didn't want to live with the thought of loving someone I couldn't be with. But last night, David said that wasn't going to happen. He says we'll see each other at breaks and vacations and talk on the phone. When he finishes law school he's going to move close to me so that we'll be together.

Together. Another wonderful word.

Dear Diary,

David is such a special person. We sat on *our* boulder and watched the sunrise this morning, then played hide-and-seek in the vineyards. We held hands and prayed together in the nine-hundred-year-old church.

We went climbing on the boulders. We made love again. And again.

I've never been this happy.

Dear Diary,

David's friend, Jerry, took off for a day of hiking. I'm glad. I still don't like him.

Meanwhile, David and I talked about what we want from life. It's amazing how close two minds can be! We both want lots of children and a big home. Family life will be our most important goal.

I was so lucky to meet him. Fate was looking out for me. He's such a loving man . . . I'm such a lucky girl. Woman.

Dear Diary,

David is gone. He left at six-thirty this morning, and he never said goodbye to me. When I went to our rock, Jerry was there, waiting, with his usual smirk. He handed me a note from David and said David was called home because of a family emergency and that he would get in touch with me later, when things calmed down. Thank goodness I wrote my address in David's journal. Only I don't have his, and I wouldn't ask Jerry for it for anything! But the note said everything I needed to know. It said *I love you and I'll call you soon. Love, David.*

Jerry made some snide comment about hoping I enjoyed my fling. I ignored him. He didn't have

David's note. I do. And he didn't realize just how close we were. He doesn't know David loves me.

I spent the day on our rock.

Dear Diary,

Every time I start packing to go home, I cry. I fold a blouse and I cry. I know it's stupid, but I can't seem to stop. David's been gone a week. Even though I'm looking forward to going home and being able to hear David's voice on the phone, nothing will really ever be the same. This time with David in Vernazza was magical.

Maybe we can come back here on our honeymoon. Oh, I know we didn't discuss it, but David and I are going to get married. It was one of those unspoken vows that both people know without having to form the actual words. We'll be very happy and perfect parents to at least four children. And very rich. David will make a terrific attorney, and I'm going to make a wonderful mother and teacher. So why am I crying?

Dear Diary,

I miss David so much. This diary was supposed to be a journal of my trip to Italy, but I've been back home two weeks and I'm still writing in it. It's the one thing I can do that I did when I was with David.

And I'm scared. I expected his letter to be waiting for me when I returned. It wasn't. Enrolling in school and getting classes and books together has kept me busy, thank goodness. I only think of David every five minutes instead of every minute.

I even called Atlanta Information last night. I asked for David's number, only to remember that he's living with his mom and stepdad, and I don't know his stepfather's last name. We should have exchanged addresses instead of my writing in his journal. But we really thought we had another week together to work out the details of how to keep in touch.

Besides, who knows? I could be jumping to conclusions. He might have lost his journal and be trying to reach me as hard as I'm trying to reach him.

Dear Diary,

I don't know what to do. It's been a month since I returned home. David hasn't called or written. I telephoned the law school he was going to attend, but he isn't registered.

I thought I knew him so well. I can't believe he lied to me. I can't believe it, but I don't know what else to think. I've heard of guys who'll say anything to get a girl into bed. We discussed the loose morals of the sixties, and seemed to agree. I guess he was just pretending. *No!* I refuse to believe that. That's more like Jerry. David was different. He knew my innermost secrets, for heaven's sake! I wouldn't have told him anything if I'd thought he was using me.

He wasn't.

I know he wasn't.

Dear Diary,

I called Mom at work and asked her to come home early tonight. Dear sweet heaven, how am I going to explain this mess? School is wonderful, but I can't continue this way. My thoughts are so topsy-turvy that all I do is cry, then call myself a fool for feeling sorry. Then I cry again. Maybe Mom has an idea I haven't come up with. I don't know what do do.

Still no word from David.

I'm going to have a baby.

1

Twenty-two Years Later

SUZANNE LANE stepped off the train and stood on the bridge overlooking the small Italian fishing village of Vernazza. She took a deep breath of air and smelled the town's unique scent: baked bread, fish, the tangy scent of wine, the dampness and the heat. It hadn't changed much. A few more houses marched a little higher on the hill. A few more people wandered the cobbled streets. There might even be a few more stores and restaurants along the winding walkway. But there were still no cars allowed on the sloping street that widened into a square at the sea's edge.

"Suzanne!" She heard Tina's voice through the children's shouts and grandmothers' gossiping drone.

Suzanne's eyes scanned the group of people on the street below before she spotted her cousin. Though she was still petite and youthful looking, Suzanne saw few signs of aging in Tina. The dark hair was now threaded with silver, which the late-afternoon sun highlighted. Her waist, thanks to four children and an obvious abundance of pizza and pasta, had filled out to match her hips. But even from this distance, the twinkle in her eyes said she was the same wonderful Tina.

Suitcase in hand, Suzanne ran down the steps and into her cousin's arms. Laughter and tears mingled as they hugged. Then Suzanne pulled away and looked hard at her cousin before hugging her again. The lump in her throat wouldn't go away.

"I've missed you," Tina admitted, breaking the emotional silence. She kissed Suzanne on the cheek again.

"I've missed you, too," Suzanne confirmed. "It's not easy when my best friend is in one country and I'm in another. One phone call a month isn't enough."

"I came back three years ago," Tina reminded her as she linked arms with Suzanne. They strolled down the street toward the restaurant and home Tina and Arturo owned by the water's edge.

"Since then, your letters have left a lot to be desired." Suzanne stared down at her cousin. "What's going on?"

Tina shrugged, evading Suzanne's eyes. "What can you expect when all of my normally intelligent children decide to go through a second childhood before they've even left their first one?"

Suzanne laughed. "Really?"

Tina nodded. "Yes, and it's been going on ever since I mentioned that I might want to visit my homeland more often. Suddenly they can't do without me for anything. For advice, babysitting, cooking, mending and a whole bunch of other, motherly duties."

Suzanne widened her eyes in surprise. Normally, Tina's children were self-reliant. "That sounds exhausting!"

"It is. I'm just about ready to strangle them." Tina's voice sounded determined. "And I'm going to start with their father, who probably put them up to it."

"I'm astounded, but if Arturo did put the kids up to it, you know he did it out of love and worry for you."

Tina sighed heavily and made a sad face. "I know. It's the only reason he's still alive."

By the time they reached the village square, both women were laughing. Standing on the steps of the old stone church in the corner of the square, a man held his breath and watched them walk through sunbeams as the late-afternoon sunlight circled them in a halo of iridescence.

Tina and Suzanne strolled slowly toward the restaurant. They edged around a group of children playing soccer, then took seats at one of the outside tables, shaded by a colorful umbrella. Suzanne gazed around, taking in the new umbrellas, the freshly washed stones, the white tables scrubbed sparkling clean. "The new restaurant looks good. And with Arturo's outgoing personality and your cooking, how could you go wrong?"

"Easily, believe me," Tina said dryly. "Most of the recipes I'm using are Mama Rosa's—with a variation, of course. But trying to second-guess the patrons and how many will show up for our gastronomic delights isn't easy or scientific."

"I thought that type of information came with experience."

"It does but good instincts help."

"Can I help?"

"No," Tina said with a laugh. "You came to see if you could write the great American novel. Isn't that why you rented the Garzolas' home for the next two months—to get away from it all, to do new things?"

"And I will, too. Being a schoolteacher, I've learned I need to vary my routine, or else boredom sets in."

"There is nothing boring about this place," Tina said. "When I first came here, I thought I must have been crazy to fall in love with an Italian and move to an out-of-the-way fishing village in a foreign country. My problem was that I equated small with boring."

"And it isn't?" Suzanne asked. She had always wondered how Tina survived in a village with only five hundred people. Although Suzanne always loved visiting, she also liked going home to New Orleans with its fast food and modern conveniences.

"Not at all. The strange thing is that sometimes I feel like a scientist looking through a microscope. This village is like a small cross section of life, and when I look through the lens, I can see all the details. I couldn't do that in New Orleans."

"My, my," Suzanne said softly, wanting to tease her cousin. "That's a great thought for someone who's under five foot tall."

Tina grinned. "Everyone always underestimates me, believing my height has something to do with the size of my brain."

"And it doesn't?"

"No, but my size does show up the lack of brain in others who believe that hogwash."

They both burst out laughing. Twelve-year-old Theresa carefully exited the restaurant doors and walked toward them. Her small hands were clamped around a tray containing two glasses filled with ice and a large bottle of cool water. After depositing the tray and hugging her aunt, Theresa skipped back indoors.

"That's all of your family I'm getting to see?"

"Arturo is inside," Tina confirmed. "He promised me a day away from all the usual household chores. I asked for peace and some private time with you, and he's giving it to me." Tina leaned closer. "But I know it's killing him. He wants to come out here and listen to all our gossip. He's as bad as any nosy fishwife."

"Think he'll come out?"

"He'd better not, under penalty of perpetual harassment."

Suzanne considered the situation. What Tina needed was a day away from the village. But she wouldn't go on her own. She would have to be coerced into it. "I'll bet you a trip to Florence, my treat, that it'll take less than fifteen minutes for him to cave in and ask to sit with us."

"You're on, as the youngsters say." Tina held out her hand. "He was so sincere about giving me this time that I doubt he'll come out here for at least an hour."

As they shook hands, Tina laughed. "I love Florence this time of year."

It was amazing, Suzanne thought. In the space of fifteen minutes the years had melted away and they were young again. They could conquer anything, do everything. But life had turned out so differently....

Tina leaned back and stretched, then lifted the damp strands of dark hair off her neck and let the breeze play against her skin. "When will Dawn and Eve be here?" she asked.

"Not until the end of the month. Dawn is having a wonderful time being big sister and introducing Eve to her Europe."

"They're good kids, Suzanne. When you divorced their dad, they were both worried about you. I got more than a few phone calls from telephone booths in high school and college."

Suzanne was surprised and touched by her daughters' concern. "I didn't know that."

"They didn't want you to know. They wanted you to feel better about yourself."

"That's why I left John. He was always my teacher, my mentor." How could she explain, even to her cousin, that her marriage had turned sour because John couldn't deal with an adult woman—in his life or bed. He wanted her to remain his eager pupil. "As I grew, I wanted to make my own decisions, and he wasn't prepared for that. John will always be a teacher—a father to whomever he's with. I didn't need that image anymore. Thanks to John I had grown, and thanks to me, I was smart enough to realize it."

"You need to explain that to your daughters."

Tina was right. Suzanne had avoided talking about the divorce with the girls. Obviously they needed to hear more. Although she and John had parted ways almost three years ago, the divorce hadn't become final until this spring. And obviously the girls had relived the same emotions she had when she had finally received the papers. "When they get through with their wanderings and come here, I will."

Tina looked down at her drink, then back up. "Has John said anything about telling Dawn about her real father?"

Suzanne stiffened. "Tina, John *is* Dawn's real father. He's been her father since she was a year old. He was up with her at night and took care of her during the day. He adopted her when she was two years old. She is John's child. End of discussion."

"All right, all right, dear. I didn't mean to get your dander up. I was just wondering if the divorce changed anything for John."

"Not at all."

Silence hung awkwardly, but when Tina asked about Suzanne's job, they seized the topic with zest.

"I love teaching teenagers. But as I told you, I want to try my hand at writing fiction. This is my summer to try it. Other than that, I couldn't be happier. Mom is doing fine. She's taking care of the house for me this summer. Her skills as a gardener are making her famous. Would you believe a stranger knocked on her door and asked if he could see her backyard?"

"And did Aunt Julia promptly show them through the house and into the backyard?"

"You bet. We'll never get her to be cautious enough to check out a person's credentials before opening the door." Suzanne sighed. "Especially now. It turns out the man is from a local magazine and wants to do a photo layout of her garden for their cover story."

"Are you going to write the copy?"

Suzanne shook her head. "Mom's garden isn't fiction, my dear cousin. My writing is."

Still smiling, Suzanne glanced up at the tall body standing beside their table, blocking the sunlight. Her first thought was that Arturo had joined them and she'd won her bet. But she immediately saw she was wrong.

The man was tall, with dark curly hair and blue eyes. Dressed in a white shirt, matching shorts and expensive tennis shoes, the strap of a leather backpack was slung over one very well-built shoulder.

She caught her breath. Her heart stopped beating.

"Suzanne?" His voice was husky, deeper than she remembered. But just as sexy and as commanding.

She wet her lips. "Yes?" she whispered, hoping—praying. This couldn't be . . . He wasn't . . .

"I'm David Marshall. Remember me?" He held out his hand to clasp hers. "We met here years ago. Twenty-two, to be exact. But never in my wildest dreams did I expect to see you here again. How lucky can I get?"

A thousand memories exploded in her head like flashbulbs, each one more blinding. She forced out her words. "David?"

He nodded, his smile bright enough to rival the sun and powerful enough to cause sunburn.

"David Marshall?"

He nodded again.

For one incredible second, all she felt was happiness at seeing David again. Then all of her memories came crashing in on her. Her heart began beating so quickly, it was like the wings of a hummingbird fluttering against her breast.

She had no smile to offer. No well-wished words. She had no other thought than to get away from him.

Extracting her hand from his, she stood. "I was just leaving," she said, hearing her voice waver. "It was nice seeing you again."

"But—"

Ignoring everything, Suzanne picked up her suitcase and walked away. Her steps were wooden, her back ramrod straight.

It wasn't until she reached the coolness of the interior that she began to shiver.

Without being told, she knew that David wouldn't let her just walk away. She had never felt so confused in her whole life.

David Marshall was here.

She craved to hold him.

She needed to scream at him.

She prayed she could hide her private truths from him.

2

SUZANNE STARED out the dining-room window, but she didn't see the colorful laundry against the pastel shades of the buildings. She didn't see the sunlight and shadows dancing on the stucco walls. She didn't even hear the stereo that was filtering classical music into the early-evening air.

Instead, her entire body was attuned to a man she couldn't see. She knew he was still standing in the piazza. Waiting.

She didn't have the nerve or the heart to face him.

Suzanne walked to the mirror on the wall next to the heavy exterior door. Staring into the glass, she saw a forty-year-old woman with clear skin, pale hazel eyes that showed the hardships of living and tiny laugh lines surrounding a wide mouth. Her hair was still light brown, but strands of gray glinted here and there. Her body was still as slender and almost as agile as it had been two decades ago. Only she knew about the battle scars of maternity lightly indenting her stomach.

Where had all the time gone? In the mirror she could see the young girl whose youthful excitement had known no bounds as she readied to meet the boy of her dreams. David.

But her heart also ached with the remembrance of the hurt that same girl had experienced when David left her.

The years, the children and her ex-husband, John, had helped soften that terrible blow. Not enough, apparently, because that ugly feeling of abandonment had returned, full-fledged. It was there in her eyes, in the tight lines around her mouth. In her heart.

Why? the young girl in her cried out. The older Suzanne still had no answer.

She had changed from being high-spirited and fun loving to grow scared and old before her time because of David. She now bore no resemblance to the girl who'd looked to the future with zest and fervor. And all because of David.

The panic she had felt at eighteen returned. She needed to hide! She needed to run away, so she would never see him again.

Her oldest daughter, Dawn, could never meet David. Suzanne wouldn't allow it. It would ruin everything.

Suzanne remembered Dawn's adolescence. When her daughter turned fourteen, it was as if she had transformed into a Mr. Hyde after being a perfect Dr. Jekyll all her young life. Suzanne had seen signs of belligerence, but she wasn't prepared for the total and unexpected mood swings from one moment to the next.

Everything Suzanne said or did was worthless or meddling—or worse yet—totally uncool. Dawn's choice of new friends were kids whose uniform was faded and holey jeans and concert T-shirts. Suzanne alternately ordered, cajoled, pleaded and begged. Nothing worked. Dawn ignored everyone, especially her parents, becoming even more wild. Had Suzanne been more experienced, less naive; more alert and less blind, she might have recognized the symptoms earlier and done something. As it was, she didn't and everything continued in a downhill spiral.

After a year or so of her abhorrent behavior, everyone was tense and ready for a fight. One word spoken loudly was enough to bring all members of the household into the fray. Eve, long a worshiper of her older sister, began crying at the drop of a hat, or pretending everything was fine when it obviously wasn't.

John was the worst. In the privacy of their room he would whisper angry words about Dawn's behavior, reminding her that obviously Dawn's real father's genes were defective, and that he was paying the price of another man's folly. Even when there was a moment of peace, his rough, hurtful words remained wedged between them—keeping them apart.

On Dawn's sixteenth birthday, she went wild. Unknown to John or Suzanne, she had expected a car for her present. She'd obviously wanted it so badly that she'd convinced herself that her parents would come through. When she received a clock radio instead, she began throwing things.

By the time her tantrum was over, so was the family as they knew it. John and Suzanne made a tough decision. They placed Dawn in a hospital for observation, only to find that their darling daughter had been using drugs. They had been too blind to see it.

Two months later, it was a different Dawn who finally returned home, but now all her anger was focused on Suzanne. The therapist had explained that this occasionally happened, and the one closest to the child was the one who received the brunt of the blame for the present circumstances.

It had taken counseling, time, perseverance, patience and love for Suzanne to keep a tenuous hold on her relationship with Dawn. Only the grace of God had seen Dawn finish high school. Suzanne felt near to bursting with pride in her daughter for catching up on her grades enough to even qualify for college, let alone graduate this past spring. Only in the last two years had Dawn and Suzanne begun to repair the damage done to their relationship. If Dawn now found out that her mother had lied about her father, their relationship would be destroyed.

Nothing was worth losing her relationship with her children. Nothing.

Suzanne felt ready to scream, then saw her cousin standing in the doorway, her brown eyes filled with concern and perhaps just a little fear.

Sobered by that thought, she demanded, "Has he ever been here before, Tina? Did you ever see him and not tell me?"

Tina shook her head. "No. Never."

Suzanne believed her. So it was just one of those accidental meetings. If David had wanted to find her, he would have visited here before. Instead, this was fate playing another cruel trick on her.

She took a deep breath and pressed her hand against her roiling stomach. Before Tina could speak again, Suzanne answered the concern in her cousin's eyes. "I'm okay. Honest. It was just a moment's panic."

Tina's shoulders relaxed perceptibly. "A moment's panic? The way you took off, I thought the bomb had dropped behind my back! You scared the life out of me!"

Suzanne tried to smile, but couldn't. "Did I make a complete fool of myself?"

"No, but it was a little awkward. After all, the guy has no idea of what's wrong. He saw an old teenage flame who ran like he's an ugly, old tom, and you're allergic to cat hair." Tina closed the door and headed toward the couch. "It's a good thing we leave our doors unlocked, or you'd be sitting out in the hall right now."

Suzanne sighed, forcing her hands to unclench. "I just didn't know what to do."

"He's a mean wolf in macho wolf's clothing," Tina decided angrily. "Don't forget, he's the one who walked out on you. Not the other way around. The louse could have called anytime in the past twenty-two years. He chose not to."

Suzanne sat down on the couch next to her cousin and stared out the window. "Are you sticking up for my actions, then and now?"

"Not in the least," Tina answered honestly. "I'm your best friend and cousin. But acting the way you did would make any man suspicious. You need to pretend indifference."

"I know," Suzanne whispered, hearing her voice break as she spoke. "I did it all wrong! I should have been cool. I should have pretended I didn't know who he was. I should have done a lot of things differently. Especially twenty-two years ago. But I didn't. So now I'll just have to repair the mistake. The next time I see him, I'll pretend I was suffering from jet lag and an upset stomach."

"Right." Tina's voice was dry. "He'll never wonder about your behavior and then your big freeze act. He'll just accept it and leave."

"You don't think so?"

"No," Tina said patiently. She turned and enveloped Suzanne's cold hands in her own warm ones.

"Then what should I do? How should I act?"

"Act as if it's nice to see him but it's no big deal, as the kids would say. Then, after you've put his suspicions to rest, you can ignore him. It'll seem like you're just not interested and don't care. It will be natural."

Suzanne struggled for calm. Tina was right. Giving David the cold shoulder would only make everything worse. Her stomach lurched again. This was no time to get sick. Right now, she had to plan out her actions. She had to pretend that David's appearance was nothing more than an odd coincidence.

She tried to smile. "Is this where all my community little theatre comes into play?"

Tina nodded, squeezing the hands she was holding. "This is it, honey. And you'll do so well, I'll probably be nominating you for an Oscar."

"Of course." Suzanne finally allowed herself to relax a little. Now that she knew what to do, she'd do it.

"Ready to have a drink with Arturo and the family? He's holding our best outside table for you. The kids are due any minute."

"I'm ready," Suzanne stated, but even to her own ears it sounded as if she were Marie Antoinette on her way to the guillotine.

As Tina stood, Suzanne gave her a hug. "Thanks, Tina."

Tina didn't pretend she didn't understand. "You're welcome. You deserve more, you know."

Arms linked, they walked out the front door. "Some ancient philosopher said that you get what you get."

Tina snorted. "Huh, some philosopher. I could have made that comment. And have. But do they pay me for my pearls of wisdom? No."

With a still-shaky stomach but a much lighter heart, Suzanne walked down the narrow steps. She pretended that everything was fine, as much for Tina's sake as for her own.

Common sense told her the hardest part was ahead. Just as had happened in the past, whatever harmed Dawn would affect Eve. Suzanne would do whatever she had to do to protect her daughters from information that could only harm them. She only hoped she was up to the task....

HANDS CLENCHED in his pockets, David stared out the window of his apartment on the top floor of an ancient, five-storied stucco house. It was perched on the edge of the bay, just below the remains of a tenth-century castle. The view was spectacular—pale blue water that reflected light like the purest jewel and the lovely old piazza. It hadn't changed much. The new additions were limited: a few new coats of paint, the railroad station and perhaps more people milling about. Directly across from his side of the piazza was the ninth-century fishermens' church. The straight, uncompromising lines and weathered, gray stone brought another, distant time and place into this century.

But the scenery didn't hold his attention. All his concentration was focused on the doorway Suzanne had disappeared into.

David couldn't have hoped for more. For twenty-two years he'd fantasized about this moment. Everything had conspired against it. In fact, he'd been sure that once he got here, he wouldn't even be able to find Tina. Who would have believed Suzanne's cousin would still be here after all these years? He'd not only found Tina, but Suzanne, too. It was a dream come true.

But why had she acted so strangely? She remembered him, that much was certain. But to leave as if she'd been . . . wounded, when only moments earlier she'd been carefree and laughing, basking in the Mediterranean sun, didn't make sense.

Could she still be angry with him for not getting in touch with her? He'd assumed she'd be more curious than angry after all this time. Twenty-two years of working, paying bills, and just plain living had passed. He was lucky that she remembered him at all. She'd been so young then. Eighteen.

A beautiful, trusting girl child.

Had Suzanne ever realized just how deeply he'd fallen in love with her? Probably not. She'd been too young to sense the depth of such emotion. He didn't know whether he regretted her lack of knowledge or was glad of it.

But, if she hadn't sensed it, then she also didn't know that he'd craved to be with her for the past twenty-two years. That he'd dreamed of her while making love to his wife. That his ambition these past few days had been to find her and either put his fantasy to rest or test the reality of a new relationship.

A family of children spilled out of the restaurant next to Suzanne's doorway. They placed dishes and glasses up on one table, then added bowls of chips and nuts and a large pitcher of what looked like sangria before sitting down around it. Their adolescent voices rose and ebbed like a human tide, blending both English and Italian.

David recalled his own young days. The oldest kid out there was probably the same age as he'd been when he arrived from college, ready to experience the Continent. The world had been his for the taking, the enjoyment, the fun of it. Everything that happened had been for his own private benefit. Nothing that didn't revolve around him mattered.

Only the young could be that cocky. That exuberant. That naive.

It had taken another young woman's shattered dreams—and his own word turned into deed—to show him what life was really about. The hardest lesson he'd had to learn was that the world revolved around the sun—not around his wishes, wants and needs.

But after twenty-two years, it was finally *his* turn. He'd earned a chance to do what he'd always dreamed of. He'd come here to try to get a lead on Suzanne. And he'd found the girl herself. Only now she was a woman—even more beautiful than she'd promised to be all those years ago.

The door to Suzanne's building opened and she stepped out with Tina at her side. Even from this distance, her gaze was clear, her full lips turned up in a smile, her good humor returned—now that he was gone? David tensed as he watched her stroll to the table filled with rowdy kids. As she kissed and hugged them, David realized the children must be Tina's family. Twenty-two years and she had at least five children. Lucky Tina. Lucky Arturo. David had always wanted a large family. So had his "Annie," as he recalled. Suzanne and he had discussed it often enough.

Suzanne hugged the youngest girl, and David wondered how many children she had. She had spent a lifetime away from him, but he knew she had not spent it alone. She was too young and beautiful. Whom had she married? Was she still married? Was she happy? These were the questions he'd teased and taunted himself with for years. Soon they would finally be answered. But for now he was content to play the voyeur.

She moved from one child to another, her laughter barely reaching him in the still afternoon air. And while he watched, he wondered how it might have been if they had lived their lives together, as they had planned. Would they still be in love today if they had spent these years together? As much in love as they'd been then? If fate had not intervened, would they now be touring Europe together? Would they be enjoying each other's company as only two people could who loved each other and possessed those small, intimate pieces of knowledge about their mate? Would her inestimable zest for life and fearlessness still be so much a part of her? Would he still crave to share those crazy, wonderful things she thought and did?

Somehow he already knew the answer to all those questions. *Yes,* his heart cried out, and at the answer tears threatened. They'd already lost so much time. Was it possible to make it up? So very much depended on her and the choices she'd made in life. For all he knew, she might have a husband waiting for her. Shaking himself to get rid of jealousy, he decided to worry about that detail later. He'd not been there for her. Instead, he'd been fighting his own dragons.

Pulling a chair up to the window, he sat back, crossed his arms and feasted his gaze on Annie. Right now he wanted to get his fill of watching a dream come true.

SUZANNE PRETENDED that nothing unusual had happened. Tina's family of children helped. In fact, Suzanne forgot about David for minutes at a time. But the threat of his reappearance was never far away and with each thought, her nerves drew tighter and tighter.

Arturo's cooking was superb. Lightly grilled fresh fish, a crispy cucumber and onion salad sprinkled with spices and olive oil, and thick, fried potatoes completed the meal. A pottery pitcher filled with local wine and of fresh fruits was constantly refilled as the children and the adults laughed and joked and caught up with the past year's activities. Even Arturo's mother and right-hand cook, Mama Rosa, slipped out from the kitchen to hug and share the close-knit family's laughter.

It was late and the three-quarter moon hung low over the Mediterranean before the clan's celebration broke up. All the restaurants in the square had closed, and only Tina's family remained to clean up the mess made by their own revelry, chattering noisily as they went back and forth between the outside table and the door leading directly to the long narrow hall of a kitchen.

After great debate, it was decided that the guest of honor could not help clean, so Suzanne was seated on the low wall next to the church and made to watch. For tonight, her nephew, Vittorio, told her, she was company. Tomorrow she could help clean the squid if she wanted to share the family duties. The mischievous glint in his eyes told her he knew she wouldn't be showing up for that duty tomorrow—or any other day.

Water lapped lazily against the ancient, gray stones of the harbor wall. The soothing, gentle sound would have relaxed her under normal circumstances. Instead, her neck tingled. She glanced around the almost deserted square. Nothing. Forcing herself to ease the tense muscles, she concentrated on the children's dialogue as they bickered back and forth between their parents and themselves.

Suzanne didn't know what finally made her look up at the darkened, open-shuttered window on the other side of the piazza. But when she did, her heart skipped a beat. David was there watching her and didn't even try to make a secret of it. As if in slow motion, he raised a hand and gave a small wave.

Automatically Suzanne waved back.

She tried to look elsewhere, pretending she didn't care he was there, even though she knew better. And she knew that he knew better. There was an invisible cord between them, pulling, tugging at her. She wondered if it pulled at him, too. Anger told her she shouldn't care. But she did. His gaze also made her aware of her every gesture, every movement. Every breath.

Making a blank of her mind, Suzanne stared across the small harbor and out to sea. The moon glowed on the calm, softly undulating waves. Her body should have relaxed, should have felt the pressures of worries seeping away. Instead, it was taut with constantly building tension.

Thoughts, no matter how hard she tried to ignore them, flooded her mind. What did he think? Did he notice the changes in her that age had wrought?

Stop it! she screamed silently. Unable to sit quietly any longer, Suzanne pushed away from the wall and walked toward Tina standing in the doorway of the kitchen.

Giving her cousin a hug, she pleaded tiredness. As the children came out of the narrow area, Suzanne gave each of them a hug and kiss, too. First the oldest, twenty-one-year-old Vittorio, with his shy but very Italian manly ways, gave her a squeeze, then blushed. The sixteen-year-old and already voluptuous Gina got her hug, followed by her thirteen-year-old sister Tatti, the twelve-year-old twins, Theresa and Tony, and last of all, shy and sweet, nine-year-old Maria.

By the time Arturo had turned out the lights and locked the door behind them, Suzanne realized she really was tired.

She never looked at the darkened window where she knew David still sat. Instead, she entered her own apartment. Keeping the rooms dark, she walked to the window overlooking the square she had just left. She brushed back the curtain and stared across the way.

He was still there. His shadow was hard to see, but to Suzanne it was as if he were outlined in neon.

Dropping the drape back into place, Suzanne undressed and slipped between the cool sheets. She closed her eyes, but sleep didn't come. Hours passed, and she was still awake. Finally she fell into a disturbed sleep filled with bizarre dreams and odd happenings.

DAVID WATCHED Suzanne's window until he felt sure she was curled snugly in her bed and sleeping soundly. Somehow it was a good feeling to know she was across the street from him, resting peacefully.

Watching her with Tina's rowdy family, he'd been struck by how wonderfully calm she was. She'd been the same way when they were young—serene and soft and so very desirable. Even back then he'd known that he could have spent the rest of his life with her. If fate hadn't interfered. But it was too late for regrets.

After stripping off his clothes, David slipped into bed and closed his eyes. Dreams of another time danced through his thoughts. Was Suzanne having the same kind of dreams? He hoped so. He fell asleep almost instantly.

SUZANNE CAME DOWNSTAIRS in the late afternoon and sat in the sun with her young second-cousins. Pretending everything was wonderful took a lot of effort. Her eyes darted constantly to the nooks and crannies of the buildings, seeking out the shadows where David might be. Watching. It was a cat-and-mouse game, one she wasn't familiar with but was willing to continue forever—if she could keep her daughter a secret.

The fear of the present mingled with the memories of the past. She remembered their meetings here. In those days she'd strolled out to the wall and looked for him. In those days she'd prayed he would show up. Now she prayed he wouldn't.

What cruel game was fate playing with her? Why did he have to reappear now? Three weeks was all they had in common. Three weeks as young adults who hadn't known what adult life was all about.

Three wonderful weeks, memories that nourished you for twenty-two-years—and a child—a little voice inside her said. She brushed the voice away, unwilling to delve into that problem.

All night she had prayed he was only here for a few days. But in her heart she knew better than to expect it. That solution was too simple.

Needing to do something constructive, she opted for a walk. Promising to return in time to dine with the family, Suzanne took the path that ran by the train station, then crossed the small parking lot up the hill to the vineyards. The scent of rain-dampened and newly tilled earth assailed her nostrils, tugging at the images she so desperately wanted to forget. She walked the spine of the hill between the rows and rows of grapevines clinging to their supports. Here and there an older woman from the village was bent over the rows of plants, weeding. Their full black skirts, peasant blouses and the kerchiefs covering their grayed heads could have been worn in the last century.

When Suzanne reached the promontory where a path branched off leading to the next village, she climbed onto a large black boulder. Circling her bent knees with her arms, she stared down at the storybook village in the canyon below.

Wedged between the mountains that rose to the sky and marched toward the land behind, God's hands had gently molded the uneven black soil and even blacker rock into a home for the fishermen who lived from the sea.

Every time Suzanne came here, she was amazed at the beauty of the countryside. Along the lower sides of the funnel, pastel stucco buildings crowded one another all the way to the piazza at the harbor. The church spire was used as a landmark by the fishermen. Across the indented harbor was another village, largest of the five towns. It sat like a jewel, but its accessibility enabled it to flourish, while Vernazza's isolation kept it as it must have been for hundreds of years. Until recently, not even a railroad had connected the town to others. A determined visitor had to drive a narrow road until they reached the edge of town. Since the medieval streets were too narrow for cars, a large public parking lot existed on top of the hill.

She took a deep breath, finally relaxing enough to smile. Tomorrow she'd start on her novel and she'd have the kind of working summer she'd always dreamed about.

And to hell—

"Does that scene bring back as many memories for you as it does for me?"

Suzanne jumped. Looking up, she was caught by smiling, intense blue eyes. "You scared me."

"I'm sorry, Annie." He didn't look the least repentant. "I didn't sneak up on you. I was coming back from Monterosso and you were sitting here." He glanced around. "You're right on the path, you know."

"I know." She returned her attention to the scenery, her mind suddenly a blank. What had happened to her plan?

"Annie," David said again. "Are you all right?"

Annie. Recollections almost overwhelmed her. No one had called her that since David had left. Until this very minute, she hadn't known she'd missed being called that.

She nodded, unable to look at him. "You must have a lot to do. Don't let me hold you up."

His chuckle skipped down her spine. "What I came to do is to find you again. And here you are."

Wide-eyed with dismay she stared up at him. "Find me? Why?"

"I needed to," he said simply. "You've been on my mind ever since I left."

Suzanne's laugh was brittle even to her ears. "I'd forgotten until I saw you yesterday," she lied. "What on earth was there to remember? That you once frolicked with a girl who had a bad case of idol worship? Or that we were too young and dumb to know we didn't have a care or worry in the world?"

His smile disappeared. "Neither. I remember the girl who was caring and loving and fun to be with. She enjoyed the same things I did. I remember summer afternoons in the sun and the scent of grapes. In the evenings, I held a girl so soft and sweet that I thought I'd already died and gone to heaven."

Deep chills invaded her. "How poetic," she scoffed. "You had such wonderful memories that they must have been all you could handle. You forgot to call or write."

"I didn't forget. I forgot I had your address in my journal. By the time I found it, fate had taken over."

Fate? Anger finally reared its ugly head. How dare he dismiss his choice on fate! "My address was inside your journal. Fate didn't make you lose it, did it?" Before he could answer, she continued. "I thought fate might have a hand in the deal, so just in case, I also gave it to your friend, Jerry. I was the one who didn't have an address. Not you."

His gaze narrowed. "So you do remember," he said softly.

"Of course," she snapped, angry with herself as well as him.

"There were reasons." His voice was soothing. "Would you like to hear them?"

She tilted her chin. She would not give him the satisfaction of letting him think she cared. "No, thank you." She pushed herself off the boulder and stood next to him.

David watched her without moving. As she began the trek down the hill, he called, "Wait!"

Suzanne mustered all the panache she could to turn and stare coolly back at him. "Yes?"

"Are you married?"

Her heart skipped a beat. "Isn't everyone?" she retorted, unwilling to discuss the marriage she'd just ended. But curiosity was a hard animal to curb. "Are you?"

"Widowed," he said and the sadness in his eyes almost broke her heart. So did the thought of how much he must have loved his wife.

"I'm sorry," she said softly.

"Don't be. She was ready. All she'd had was a life of pain."

She would not ask. She would not ask. She would *not* ask! "Pain?"

He nodded. "Annie?"

"Yes?"

"You're as beautiful as you ever were."

"Goodbye, David." She turned and began again the long walk down the hill. Suddenly she was running down the hill as fast as her heart and legs could carry her. The wind blew through her hair and caressed her skin. Her blood pumped furiously through her body. It felt wonderful. She didn't know if she was running away from David or toward whatever life had to offer next.

But for whatever reason, she felt more exhilarated than she had felt in years.

It felt so good to be alive!

Vernazza, Italy

I arrived in Vernazza yesterday and in a short twenty-four-hour period, I've been thrown into chaos. David is here. He says he came to see me. I don't know why, but I do know he will never get any closer to me than he was this afternoon. I came here to write and that's exactly what I'm going to do. Besides, I'm a grown woman now. And these confused feelings of being an adolescent again will pass. I promise. First thing tomorrow I will begin my writing.

I promise.

3

SUZANNE DIDN'T SEE DAVID for the rest of the day, but it wasn't for lack of trying. She wanted to get their confrontation over with so she could continue with her life—alone but secure.

After dinner with Tina's family, Suzanne begged off and escaped to her own quarters. For the first time since she arrived, she took the time to look around her rented apartment. The Garzolas' oldest son had invited his family to Chicago. He'd wanted them to meet his new American bride and to see how successful his business, a garage that specialized in Porsche cars, was. Their apartment gave Suzanne both privacy and a closeness with her cousin's family for the two months she was going to be here.

The Garzolas' home was much like all the other apartments in town. Since the sea occasionally flooded the lower areas of the town, the first floor of all the buildings around the plaza were shops or storage rooms. The first floor was actually the second, consisting of a large dining area and kitchen. The next floor up was a living area, filled with books and games. It was easy to imagine the family sitting around playing Italian Monopoly or putting together a thousand-piece puzzle like the partially completed one scattered on a small table in the corner. The top floor held the two bedrooms and bath. Suzanne shook her head. They had raised four children in this small apartment. In her neighborhood in New Orleans, her neighbors would call this type of living deprived. There was no icemaker, disposal, dishwasher or built-in Jacuzzi—or any of the other gewgaws Americans considered necessities. Suzanne hated to admit it, but she envied the Garzolas. They were a loud, rowdy family who seemed to love both each other and life.

She had always wanted to belong to a large family instead of being an only child. Her parents had somehow made her feel excluded rather than part of a whole. Oh, she knew her parents had loved her very much. Her mother had helped her work through the emotional devastation of her divorce. Suzanne doubted if she would have solved her problems as well without her mother. But she still had craved the larger family and the interaction that she'd seen others enjoy.

As a child, she'd been alone so much she found it easier not to rely on others or even to want to be part of a group. But that didn't mean the longings weren't deep inside her, waiting to be fulfilled.

And when she met David, those dreams had blossomed again. They would have a large family together. She'd been going to teach school and she had.

He was going to be an attorney. Was he? Had he had those four children they had dreamed of? Had he been happily married? The answer was yes, if his expression when he had talked about his wife was any gauge.

Once again she was plagued by questions. This time, Suzanne vowed, she would receive answers. After all, they were both adults. They shared a small piece of history and it only seemed right that they should catch up—as old friends would—and find out what had happened in the ensuing years.

She jumped guiltily at the knock on the door, as if thinking about David was treason enough. But it was only Tina's youngest daughter, Maria.

"Mama said to give you this," she said shyly, holding out a letter. "And she said to remind you that we're having Grandma Rosa's pizza for dinner tonight."

Suzanne smiled. Maria's slight Cajun accent was delightful and unexpected. She bent down and kissed the child's cheek, earning a grin that would melt the hardest heart. "Thank you, Maria. Tell your mother I still love pizza and I'll be down. What kind is it?"

"Margarita," she answered, her eyes widening. "It's my favorite!"

"I'll be there," Suzanne promised again before watching the child skip down the stairs and disappear into the narrow street below.

She walked back to the window and stared out. She was lucky, she reminded herself. She had a job she loved, relatives who helped and supported, children she adored and time to try a second vocation. Nothing and no one would ruin her time in Vernazza. He'd leave soon, and she would have the rest of the summer to play in the sun and write her novel.

She picked up the mail that one of Tina's children had delivered to her earlier and discovered one was a postcard from her daughter.

Fell in love with Pompeii. Both of us cried all the way through the tour. Naples is wonderful and yet sad. Capri is totally awesome. You can get a tan without bikini lines! Can't wait to see you next month and tell you all the wonderful and zany things that have happened to us. And to think that you thought we were safe because Dawn knew the ropes! Love to Tina and cousins.

Love to you, too, Mom. Eve and Dawn

SUZANNE LOOKED FORWARD to seeing her daughters again—they were growing up so quickly. Why, in the fall Eve was beginning college, while Dawn was starting a career in accounting in Baton Rouge, an hour and a half from home.

Her elder daughter was not only a grown-up twenty-one, she was behaving like a responsible adult. Dawn was a far cry from the teenage Dawn. What Suzanne had called the "terrible times" was behind them. Dawn's rebellious attitude had disappeared slowly, inch by inch, until this past year was how Suzanne had always hoped it would be to have a grown-up daughter. The specter of the past was slowly fading, replaced with new, finer days.

Now she and Dawn were beginning a new relationship—one based on friendship, trust and love. It was still a mite touchy, but they were both trying to cope with the new status.

David was Dawn's father. Her *biological* father, she corrected. John was Dawn's father in every other way. She and John had met when she was pregnant and when Dawn was a year old, Suzanne had married him. Dawn believed her real father had died before she was born, and Suzanne had never corrected that impression. To tell the truth now would tear the bonds they had worked so hard to create.

She loved both her children, but was more protective of Dawn. A close friend, a psychiatrist, had once told her she was so overprotective because of the circumstances surrounding Dawn's birth. Suzanne had lived her lie for a long time, and would continue to maintain it if that was what it took to maintain her loving relationship with her elder daughter.

No, she would never allow David to intrude upon her world.

DAVID STOOD on the castle wall and gazed down at the village below. The scene before him could have been a travel poster.

This was the place he'd found the love of his life. This was the same place that he'd found her a second time. The pull, that commanding draw he felt for her was as strong as ever. Did she feel it, too?

But the gods were not done playing their games with him—she belonged to someone else. How could he feel so strongly about a married woman? When would his conscience kick in? Right now he felt no guilt, no worry. The only emotion he still felt was desire.

His gaze narrowed on her window far below. A shadow moved. His Annie was home.

Annie, come to me.

David was afraid to say the words aloud. For years he'd dreamed of her. Wished for her.

At first he'd thought seeing Annie standing in the piazza was a figment of his imagination. Even so, his reaction to her had been the same as it had been twenty-two years ago. Strong and with such a forceful desire, he didn't know where yearning left off and Annie began.

Suddenly the object of his thoughts stepped out of the doorway of her apartment. She couldn't see him, but he wished she did. He also wished he was down there instead of at least twenty climbing minutes away.

He watched her as she walked into the old church. Without thinking twice, he began to crawl down the side of the wall to the stony ground below. With any luck she'd be in there a while. And when she came out, he'd be waiting.

"CARE FOR a glass of the local wine?" David lifted the carafe he'd ordered just moments ago. After climbing down the hill and finding a spot where he could way-lay Suzanne when she walked out of the old stone church, he'd been saying his own prayers for good luck.

"I'd love one," Suzanne said, taking a seat across from him at the outdoor restaurant, allowing the large umbrella to shield her face from the afternoon rays. She'd known he'd be here when she came out. Unsure of how, but she did. Perhaps it was the prayer she'd said in the ancient fishermen's church.

He passed her a filled glass and she sipped the golden liquid. Light and fruity, it was the taste that Vernazza wine was quickly becoming famous for.

"What are you thinking?" His voice was low and warm and she loved the sound of it.

Suzanne glanced up and his blue eyes held hers. "Why?"

"I'm fascinated."

"Daydreams," Suzanne answered honestly.

"Of what?"

"This and that," she hedged. "Tell me what you're doing here."

"Looking for you."

"Seriously?"

"Seriously."

"Why?"

"Because I needed to."

Suzanne couldn't think of anything to say. To delve into that subject might bring up too many memories she wasn't sure she wanted to deal with quite yet.

Her best defense was to change the subject. "Did you become an attorney?"

"You remembered," David commented, and she felt herself blush. "Yes, I did, although I delayed law school for a year. Now I have my own practice with three partners. We specialize in oil royalties and contracts."

"That must be . . ." She didn't know what to say.

"Boring. I know. To most people it is." He grinned and Suzanne was instantly reminded of the young man she had known. "But I love it."

"Doesn't your practice depend on oil prices?"

He shook his head and light glinted off his hair like sunshine on a raven's wing. "Not really. Either we're working on corporate contracts and wells that are opening, or we're closing the accounts."

"That sounds . . ."

His laughter was deep and husky. "I know. Boring. My son says the same thing."

She should have been prepared for that piece of information. She couldn't explain why the thought of him having another child hurt. After all, this wasn't the boy she'd known so long ago. This was a man who had lived, just as she had, in the ensuing years. "You have a son?"

"Jason. He's visiting the French Riviera right now. I promised him a trip to Europe for his high school graduation, but I'm here in case he needs me." David's chuckle vibrated down her spine. "Although I honestly believe he'd probably enjoy himself more if he knew I was across an ocean."

She refused to acknowledge the jealousy that stirred. So what if he'd married and had a child? She had done the same, hadn't she? But she had never really been content. Obviously he was. That was enough to be jealous about.

She cleared her throat. "Is he going to follow in his father's footsteps and become an attorney?"

"No. He wants to be a psychologist. He believes attorneys are the plague of the earth."

"Ah," Suzanne murmured, sympathizing with him. His Jason and her Eve had a lot in common. Eve was as opinionated as only an eighteen-year-old could be. Only she wanted to be a Special Education teacher so she could help others.

"You sound as if you know what I'm talking about. Do you have children?"

She leaned back in her chair, as if doing so would keep him from finding out anything she didn't want him to know. "Yes." She spoke cautiously. "I have two daughters."

David twirled his wineglass on the tabletop, staring at it instead of her. "And do they look like you or your husband?"

She watched him cautiously. "My oldest, Dawn, looks like her father. My youngest looks like me," she managed at last.

He finally glanced at her. A slow, sad smile turned his lips up. "I bet they're both beautiful." He covered her hand with his. The touch sent tingles through her body.

"Of course," she murmured. She cursed herself as she blinked away the tears that threatened to film her eyes. It was hard not to recall how she had tried to find him, tried to let him know that he had a beautiful baby daughter.

"Oh, Annie," he said softly. "I wish we could have been together. I would have loved to watch you change."

Afraid of her own reaction to both his touch and his pet name for her, she withdrew her hand. "I've grown enough, thank you," she said, trying to make a joke of it. But it didn't work.

"You certainly have," he repeated. "And you're more beautiful than ever."

She refused to respond. She had no interest in a flirtation.

"How long will you be here?"

She placed her wineglass carefully on the table. "Several weeks," she prevaricated. "How long are you staying?"

"Two weeks. I promised Jason two weeks in Europe."

"Oh." Tension released its hold on her body. Two weeks. He'd be gone before her girls arrived. He'd never know....

"Have dinner with me tonight."

Afraid to look at him, Suzanne stared down at the carafe. Why not? He was here and she enjoyed his company. He was single, she was, too—although he didn't know that.

Temptation was too great. "I'd love to."

"Good. I'll pick you up about seven-thirty."

"I'll meet you down here."

David shook his head. "I'll pick you up. In case you didn't notice, this is a date."

Her heart skipped a beat at the word—just as it had when she was a teenager. "I'm sorry. I didn't realize. It's been quite a while since I've gone through this ritual," she teased. "Is there anything else I should know?"

"No. Except that I'm allowed to open doors, lead you to the table, pull out your chair and give you a chaste good-night kiss."

She raised her brows in an attempt to look cool and controlled, but her heart hammered against her breast at the thought of a kiss—chaste or not. "All that?"

"All that." His smile was engaging, but his blue eyes held flecks of steel that told her he meant all that—especially the kiss.

Suzanne stood up and smiled. "Well, thank you for the wine, but I've got to get some things done if I'm going to be ready for all that."

"See you then."

His intense gaze heated her skin all the way to her door. When she was in the shadowed stairway, she finally let out her breath.

Muscles suddenly turned to Jell-o. She had to relax. Now that she knew that he'd be gone in two weeks, she could enjoy his company. Wasn't it every woman's dream to find the first love in her life and see what had happened to him?

And wasn't it also every woman's dream to be loved from her youth right into old age—if forty could be considered the gateway to old age?

Her only problem was that she could not discuss Dawn. That was going to be hard, since her children were so much a part of her life. She'd be flirting with disaster, but it was a chance she'd take. He'd be gone before anything could happen.

She remembered the silver-framed photograph of the girls, hurried to the buffet in the dining area and took the picture off the shelf. This would really give the game away!

DAVID WATCHED ANNIE until she disappeared inside the building. Exhilaration flowed through his body. He felt as if he were dancing on the edge of a live volcano. Annie was having dinner with him tonight.

He gulped down the last of the wine in his glass, but his excitement level was already at fever pitch. What was it about the woman that put his entire system into turmoil? He was afraid he knew what it was called. Love was too permanent a word; it brought to the fore all the feelings he'd thought were dead.

After pouring another glass of wine, he leaned back and stared out at the pure blue undulating water. The heat of the summer sun felt good against his skin. Suddenly he felt young. Miraculously, the clock had been turned back, giving him the vitality of youth. That same transformation also granted him the indecision of adolescence, but he could cope with that. At least some of his experience would help.

One thing he did know. This was a twenty-two-year-old fantasy. He might be older, but he sure as hell wasn't the worse for wear—and he was going to prove that to Suzanne.

"STUNNING!" David's gaze skimmed her body approvingly.

"Thank you," she murmured, feeling the heat of a light blush touch her cheeks. "Won't you come in?"

When he stepped inside the room, it seemed as if half the oxygen left. Her own breath became light and airy. "A glass of wine?" she asked.

"I'm not thirsty," he admitted with a smile. "I sat downstairs and had a glass of mineral water while I waited for the time to pass."

He stepped closer and her gaze locked on his mouth. "Would you like to discuss the merits of bottle waters and wines?"

"No." Her voice was almost a whisper. His smile was so endearing. He was so close.

"Don't you think we ought to get it over with?" he asked, his voice low and smooth.

"It?"

"Our kiss."

His breath caressed her cheek, and for a moment she had to close her eyes as one erotic image after another invaded her mind. "I don't remember asking for one," she finally managed.

"Neither did I. I just thought that since we're both feeling awkward because we haven't kissed, it would be best to get it out of the way. Then we can set about having a good time without that worry hanging over our heads."

"Is it hanging over your head?"

Blue eyes stared down at her. He nodded slowly. "Like the sword of Damocles."

"Well," she said softly. "That sounds too precarious to me. We'll get this one kiss out of the way and then we can get on with our evening."

Lightly calloused fingertips stroked her arms, caressing her shoulders before he pulled her toward him with excruciating slowness. "Right," he drawled, then brought his head down.

His lips touched hers and her breath caught in her throat.

She was afraid to move. David might pull back and end their touch. Her hands brushed his broad shoulders and etched the corded muscles beneath her fingertips.

The pressure of his mouth increased slightly and her body flowed into the hard contours of his, filling the muscle-hardened gaps and spaces with her own femininity and softness. Her arms crept around his neck and she held on as if going on a roller-coaster ride. Her lashes fluttered once, twice, then gave in to the sensation that had nothing to do with sight. Her hands, her skin, her mouth could do that for her.

David hadn't changed. In fact, he'd become more potent. Memories of youth came back. Magnified. Intensified. She clung harder to his shoulders.

She could feel his touch on her arms tremble before he circled her waist and pulled her even closer. He captured her tongue and dueled ever so gently until she allowed him to win.

He felt rock hard and hot. He held her as if she might escape or melt in a puddle on the cool tile floor.

She was unprepared for the desolate feeling that flooded through her when he pulled away in obvious reluctance. His forehead touched hers as their breath mingled in the small space between them.

"Some things get better with age." He looked as affected by their kiss as she was.

"Good wine and what?" she asked, equally breathless. She leaned back and looked up at him. With a shaky finger, Suzanne traced the hairline at his temple. She needed to continue touching him—to keep the contact. Closing her eyes, she took a deep gulp of air and prayed her heart would cease its frantic beating soon.

"And you," he said, bending toward her and placing a light kiss on the sensitive side of her hand. Heat filled her arm. "Definitely you."

"And you, too," she whispered.

"I remember kissing you a thousand years ago. Your touch was just as powerful then." He sighed, and his warm breath stroked her skin. "You were always a potent weapon, Annie."

Her laugh was shaky, she knew. "It's just a response to the past. That's all."

David's blue eyes narrowed. "Do you honestly believe that?"

She nodded. "Of course. It's just a teenage fantasy that finally played itself out. That's all."

His grin was knowing. "Liar. But that's a topic for another time."

Realizing how close they still were, she stepped back, out of his clasp. His arms dropped to his sides and she hoped that he felt as chilled by her absence as she was by his.

Full of regrets and more unanswered questions, she asked, "Are we ready? I'm starving."

"We're ready and I'm glad you're hungry. I've had the chef fix a little something special for us."

"Anything I can pronounce?"

He chuckled. "We'll see. Meanwhile, the view awaits."

As they walked out the door and down the stairs, Suzanne wondered if they were thinking about the same view. She could stare at him all night long.

Maybe this time she could get him out of her system. . . .

4

THE CASTLE POINT was ablaze with the colors of sunset. Without the sun's brilliant light, the water was inky black, the rocks even blacker. Someone in the small village had a stereo turned high and an aria drifted on the evening air.

Crisp wine, chilled bottled water and a fish hors d'oeuvre were already on the table. David had ordered their meal ahead of time, so Suzanne had nothing to do but enjoy the scenery around her. Her choices were limited. It was either that or stare at her dinner partner. If she did much more of the latter, he might get the idea she was ready to dine . . . on him.

"I always dreamed of being up here with you."

Suzanne looked down. His gaze was too intense. Then she belatedly remembered that she didn't want him to realize how much he unsettled her, so she looked him in the eye. "Twenty-two years ago, this restaurant wasn't here."

One brow rose in an arrogant gesture, and Suzanne caught a glimpse of an intimidating legal advisor across a negotiating table. "I didn't dream of sitting in a restaurant. I always imagined you alone with me and the Mediterranean." His gaze skimmed her body before returning to the softness of her eyes. "Even then I was jealous of the breeze touching your skin."

"How romantic," Suzanne murmured, unnerved by the intensity of his words. Her only defense was to try to make light of their date.

"You're nervous."

"Yes."

"Why?"

She didn't know where the words came from, but once she started, she couldn't stop. "You're so intense. Even when you're relaxing, you're intense. I don't know what you see when you look at me, but I get the feeling you're seeing more than I want you to."

"Do you have a guilty conscience about something? Are you afraid of exposing secrets? Desires?"

"No." She knew she'd denied it too vehemently. Purposely calming herself, she continued. "It's the reaction of any private person."

"You are very private, aren't you?" He took a sip of his drink for the first time. "I never thought of you that way before."

"I'm reserved." She'd changed so much. The youthful zest and eagerness to meet challenges head-on was gone.

"Tell me about your life."

She wanted to. Oh, how she wanted to! Instead she remained cautious. "When I graduated from college, I began teaching. I love it, but it's tiring. I already told you I have two daughters. They're both charming and outgoing and all the other things I wanted to be when I was in school. We still live close to where I grew up. New Orleans holds a fascination for me, although I think I could do without the humidity."

"How old are your girls?"

Was it wrong to lie? A very small lie? She would do whatever it took to keep the information from David. "One is twenty and one is eighteen."

"It's a shame you didn't bring them with you."

Suzanne breathed a sigh of relief. It was going to be all right. "Yes. They would have loved visiting with Tina's family. Tina and Arturo have only been to New Orleans once with their family, but our children all got along wonderfully. In fact, Dawn and Vittorio are very close friends."

"Vittorio is Tina's oldest?"

Suzanne nodded. "Yes. They're close in age, and Vittorio stayed with us while attending college in Louisiana with Dawn."

"And your husband? What's he like?"

Another lie. How many would she tell? she wondered. "He's a geologist in oil and loves it. When the girls were growing up, they knew more about rock formations than sewing and cooking." Memories of those days flooded her and the nostalgia made her smile. They had been good days.

"Do you love him?"

Her startled gaze flew to his. This time she refused to lie and stared out to sea.

Luckily the waiter filled the silence, arriving to serve plump, handmade pillows of ravioli in a spinach and cream sauce. For a while they enjoyed the lack of conversation. Birds sought their nests in the trees and craggy rocks, the water slowed its lapping rhythm against the shore. The evening turned cooler. A string of gay lights bobbed in the easy summer breeze, dimly lighting the stone patio around them.

Finally David broke the silence. "Maybe we can get your kids and Jason together sometime. I think they'd all get a kick out of that. I know Jason would."

"Why? You don't even know us."

"I've spoken to Jason about you, Suzanne. He knows you and I were in love when I visited here after college." He leaned back in his chair. "And he knows I was coming here to see if I could pick up your trail and perhaps find you again."

Her heart cried out at the futility of it. If only he'd been there when Dawn was little. Not now. Dear sweet heaven, not now! "Sometimes old ghosts need to die a peaceful death. Besides, there must have been many women in your life after Europe."

David crossed his arms over his broad chest. "What makes you say that?"

"You never called me, but you married and had a son after leaving here."

"When we were young and in love, Annie, I didn't tell you everything. In fact, there were several things I should have stated right up front."

The tone of his voice sent chills down her spine. "What kind of secrets did you have at twenty-one?"

"Hard to believe that a kid that age could have a few secrets, isn't it?" His laugh was gruff. "And the more I carried them around without telling you, the guiltier I felt. But I knew that as soon as I took care of the emergency at home, I'd call and explain, and everything would be okay again."

"Did your friend, Jerry, know your secret?"

David nodded. "Yes."

"So, at last." Suzanne's voice sounded hard, even to her ears. "The mystery will be solved."

"I wanted to be on your doorstep the week of your return to the States and carry you off."

"Only if you had my permission," Suzanne bluffed. Her heartbeat refused to stay controlled. So many lives would have been different if he had done that.

His look told her that he doubted he'd have needed her permission. "Back then we thought the same."

She didn't deny his claim. She'd been a fool then, but at least she recognized it. Now she was caught in a different web, and it didn't matter how she felt about David.

"Maybe," she hedged. "Tell me what happened to your honest intentions."

"Annie, when I met you I was engaged."

She felt the earth drop away. Her fingers gripped the table for balance. "Formally?"

He nodded. "I had given her an engagement ring the day of my graduation in June of that year. I didn't know that in August I'd meet a woman who would make me see everything differently—including who I wanted to marry." His gaze was so filled with pain, it seemed to spill over into her own soul. " We were childhood sweethearts. Barbara and I lived down the street from each other. We were partners in junior high dance class. We attended every homecoming dance and prom together. We graduated from high school and college together. We were best friends."

Suzanne's heart felt as if it was going to break. He'd already had someone when he came here to take advantage of her. Anger swelled inside her breast. He'd already had a girl! She hadn't stood a chance!

"We decided to get married at Christmas, during law school break, when she wouldn't be teaching."

Her heart sank even further. "She taught school?"

"Yes. High school English."

She blinked away the tears. Not now. Not until she was back in her apartment and had privacy. Then she could cry all night.

"You must miss her very much," she finally managed after swallowing the thick lump in her throat.

"I do. And Jason misses her more. He doted on his mother, even helped take care of her when I was away on business."

"How sad." Her food sat precariously on her stomach. The wine tasted like vinegar. She needed, desperately needed, to get away from David.

Suzanne pushed back her chair. "David, I hope you don't mind. I'm not feeling well. I need to lie down a while."

"Suzanne, wait," he began, standing and reaching for her.

She was quicker, slipping from his outstretched hand and heading toward the stairs. "Please," she said quickly. "Finish your dinner. I'll talk to you later, when I feel better. I promise."

"Suzanne, don't," he said, but even he knew there was no way to halt her flight. She practically flew down the steps.

He'd been *engaged*. And he'd made love to her. Got her pregnant with Dawn. And then he'd taken off, going back to live with his wonder woman while Suzanne was left alone—with their child.

Once she was in her apartment, safe, she couldn't resist the urge to walk to the window and stare out at the castle restaurant across the way. David stood outlined against the night sky. She shivered. He reminded her of a devil preparing for his next assault.

Hearing herself cry like a wounded animal, Suzanne moaned into the darkness. The moans became deep, rasping sobs that shook her very soul.

She didn't know when she sat down on the floor or how long she stayed there. It felt as if sandpaper was under her eyelids. Her throat was raw. Her head throbbed.

How childish—and childlike—she had been! All the time she was fantasizing about their life together, his fiancée was making arrangements for a Christmas wedding! Her Christmas had been quite different. She'd spent it at home, five months pregnant with David's child and wondering why he hadn't called.

Now she knew.

She wasn't surprised by the knock on her door. She glanced at the slim black watch on her wrist. David had given her an hour to adjust to his news. Now he probably expected to pick up where they left off.

Surprise, surprise. It wasn't possible.

Feeling as if every nerve in her system was numb, she stood and walked to the door. David was leaning against the jamb, hands in pockets, a scowl marring his brow.

He muttered an expletive under his breath as he took in the ravages of tears. Pulling away from the jamb, he reached out and enveloped her in his arms.

Still numb, she let him. It took less effort than pulling away. His breath warmed her temple, his hands lightly rubbed her shoulders and back.

She felt cold. So very cold. Her heart was pumping ice water through her veins.

David murmured something again, but she didn't listen. Her entire attention was focused, like a giant floodlight inside her mind, searching the corners, nooks and crannies for all the times she had acted like a fool. Too many times. Far too many times.

David finally pulled back and stared down at her. "I haven't finished with you."

"That's odd. What else could you possibly add to this story to make it any better?" she asked, keeping her voice in a monotone.

"Plenty." His tone was grim as he led her over to the small couch. He sat down, pulling her with a deft movement into his lap as he did so.

"Go ahead. Say the rest and get this over with." Suzanne whispered, wishing she didn't smell his after-shave and that indescribable scent that was his alone. His hands knew just the right, soothing pressure to exert on her back and arms.

"I loved you, Annie," he said softly. She hadn't expected that.

Suzanne looked up at him, finally letting her eyes show some of her anger. "Keep your lies to yourself! If you'd loved me, you would have told me the truth."

"I didn't mean to, but I did fall in love with you," he insisted. "And from that point on, everything went haywire."

"No kidding."

"Remember when we met?" he asked softly. "We took walks and talked about books and records and dreams. You loved to challenge my thinking when you thought I was wrong. I loved that."

"How kind of you."

He continued, ignoring her sarcasm. "I didn't plan to become romantically involved with you. Or at least that's what I told myself," he amended. "I pretended that everything was fine and we were just friends. But Jerry knew I was falling in love with you."

"That's wonderful," Suzanne replied in the flat tone she'd used earlier. "You denied falling in love with me, but you didn't deny yourself the pleasure of making love with me. In your own words, you made love to a woman you didn't even think you loved."

His expression turned granite hard. "That's not the way it was, and you know it."

Suzanne pulled away from his clasp and stood up, placing her hands on her hips as she leaned over him. "That is right. You're just trying to dress up doing such a despicable thing in satin and lace. It's not working, David! Not with me."

He finally snapped. All his understanding was gone, and anger and frustration took its place. "Look who's talking! You're not claiming unrequited love, are you? You didn't waste any time finding a replacement for me. You went home and married immediately! It wasn't as if you gave a damn about our relationship! If you had, you would have called or written me!"

That hit hard. Her hand over her stomach, she took a deep breath before answering. "And how was I supposed to do that? You never gave me your address or telephone number!"

His body went still. David's blue eyes widened, then narrowed in disbelief. "Jerry gave you my address. He told me so."

"He lied."

"I don't believe you."

She swallowed hard. "I don't care whether you believe me or not. I know what I did, and I tried everything I could to reach you. I didn't know your stepfather's name, so I couldn't get ahold of you that way. You weren't registered at the law school you said you were attending. I waited for you to call or write. *My* address and phone number was in your journal."

His blue eyed gaze lost its hardness. "I knew exactly where it was. I stared at it so often, I know it by heart."

Suzanne crossed her arms. "Right. You looked at it so much, you dialed it in your sleep."

"555-2391."

She closed her eyes, then opened them again. "Then why didn't you call?"

David ran a hand through his dark hair. He stood and walked to the window. "I went home because Barbara had been involved in an auto accident and wasn't expected to live."

The intense pain she heard in his words washed over her, overwhelming her like a tidal wave.

"I thought that as soon as she recovered, I would tell her about you. I even told our parents about you. They weren't happy, but felt there was nothing they could do to persuade me differently. Instead, Barbara remained in a coma for three weeks. I was so worried, I practically lived at the hospital. I guess, like all people in tight situations, I made hourly deals with God. If He saved Barbara, I would do this or that. By the time two weeks had passed, I was punchy. But I couldn't call you. I promised myself that as soon as I could tell Barbara about you, then I would. And my reward would be to hear your voice. But I couldn't do that until I made sure I'd done everything in the world to insure that Barbara would be all right."

"Dear sweet heaven," Suzanne breathed.

"When she finally regained consciousness, she couldn't remember much of anything except the plans for the wedding. She had been returning from a bridal store when she was broadsided by a drunk driver. So we discussed our plans while I waited for her to get better. But she didn't. She was paralyzed from the hips down and would never walk again. The nerve damage to her back was too severe to repair itself."

Suzanne felt numb. "So you got married."

"Yes," he replied quietly. "Barbara was my best friend. We had an obligation to each other that went deeper than love. It was a bond of background, secret dreams and time. In retrospect, I think that if I had turned my back on her it would have been like rejecting my own family."

"Wasn't that tough to base a marriage only on a friendship?" she asked, wondering if that was what she'd done, too.

"No. Some people go all their lives and never have the depth of friendship Barbara and I had. I'm sorry for them. They'll never know the value—given or received—of a friend. Although it may not be love in the traditional sense, it's a commitment of the soul, just the same. And that means you never want anything to hurt or harm the other."

He turned to face her once more. The space between them seemed like miles rather than a few short feet. "I told her about you."

"You *told* her?"

His smile was wry. "I didn't have a choice. Jason was thirteen years old and had just won an award for being the best athlete of the year in his class. I was so proud of him I could have burst. And he'd been admitted to the National Honor Society. Barbara was changing clothes for the ceremony and overheard her mother saying I should be glad I hadn't ended our engagement."

"Dear sweet heaven," Suzanne murmured once again, feeling the hurt and anguish both must have experienced. She understood only too well the disillusionment of love, both from her point of view and from Barbara's. They had a lot in common. "What did she say?"

David laughed ruefully. "What could she say? She said she'd always suspected that there was someone else, but she'd been ignoring it for all those years. She said I should have asked out of our engagement, because all she really wanted was my happiness. Then she asked me if I wanted a divorce."

The story was heartbreaking. Suzanne watched David, unable to take her eyes off him. His eyes filled with tears. He didn't seem to mind that she could see them. One straggled down the length of his jaw and she longed to hold him and wipe it away. But she couldn't. She had suffered, too.

"What did you tell her?" she finally managed to ask.

"The truth," he stated unequivocally. "I told her I wouldn't have changed the past for anything. That I loved her and I was lucky to be a part of her life." His gaze was honest and unwavering. "And I meant every word. Despite the fact that I hadn't given her all my love, she had given me hers and I was lucky to share my life with her. Jason was lucky to have her as a mother. She was the sweetest, most courageous and giving woman I've ever known."

Suzanne felt the wetness of her own tears touching her cheeks, but didn't know if she was crying for Barbara, David or herself.

At last she asked the question that had been on her mind ever since he had begun to tell his story. "How did she die?"

David rubbed the back of his neck. "Two winters ago, she caught a cold she couldn't seem to shake. It turned into pneumonia. She died three weeks later. They said her stamina wasn't there. Twenty-two years of living in a wheelchair had taken its toll. She had stopped exercising, claiming that no matter what she did, she'd still be in a wheelchair."

Something in Suzanne snapped. With a heart as heavy as his, she wrapped her arms around his waist. She held him close, her hands gently soothing his back and shoulders. They both needed the touch of understanding and knowing the other cared. She wanted to ease his pain, and this was the only way she could think of to do it. Holding him was as natural as breathing.

It was as if she'd pushed a button and allowed a dam to burst. His shoulders shook with sobs that came from the soul. Tears streamed down her own face as she felt the heartbreaking rhythm of his despair.

His tears finally stopped, but still they held each other as if there were no one else left in the world except them. His warm breath caressed her cheek and shoulder. They needed each other. In an odd way, Suzanne felt as if comfort and solace could only come from him. Her hands still smoothed across his shoulders, her fingers saying all the words she wouldn't say aloud. *Couldn't* say aloud.

She didn't know how they got there, but both of them were in the center of the living area one moment, then the next minute walking in the hall and going up the stairs to her bedroom.

It felt so *right*.

A small portion of Suzanne seemed to be watching from a distance. She wasn't surprised at her own actions; in fact, she'd often dreamed about making love to David over the years. She wasn't embarrassed, either. Going to her bedroom with David seemed like the most natural thing in the world. And being together right now was another way to assuage the pain both had suffered.

Moonlight softly flooded the room through the skylight. Suzanne could see David as clearly as if the room were filled with a thousand candles. Her hands were steady as she undid the buttons of his knit shirt and tugged it gently from the waistband of his slacks. When she reached for the button, he placed his hands over hers and stilled her action. "Are you sure about this, Annie?" he asked, his voice rough, filled with the same need that was in her, demanding satisfaction. "Don't come to me out of pity."

"I'm not."

His slow smile matched hers. "In that case," he murmured in a whisky-low voice, reaching for her blouse buttons, "may I do the honors?"

"Be my guest." Her voice was breathless from the slowly building tension his touch created inside her. She felt happy and excited and loving and wanting and needing and . . .

Her blouse open and pushed aside, David's fingertips explored the full roundness of her breasts. She
held her breath as he skimmed lightly over their softness, then outlined the dark areolae until they puck-
ered with anticipation. "So very responsive," he
whispered. "So very beautiful. More beautiful than I
remembered."

"Turnabout's fair play." She lifted his shirt. With an
impatient movement, David finished the job and
threw the offending garment onto the floor behind
him. Then his hands began their exploration again.

He brushed aside her hair to stroke her neck, following the line of shadow to the center curves, then
continued down to her waist. Her breath caught in her
throat as she watched his blue eyes turn black with
passion while his hands continued their foray.

"You're so beautiful." He stared down at her, lock-
ing his gaze with her heated eyes. "Do you like to be
touched?"

"I love *you* touching me."

"Touch me," he requested in a hoarse whisper.

Her fingers trailed from the top of one broad
shoulder, over a tiny male nipple and through the
dark hair on his chest that arrowed down below the
waistband of his pants.

They reached for the waistbands at the same time,
each doing the other, then finishing their own. Still
they stood in the center of the room. The moon

poured through the skylight, painting their bodies with a silvery shimmer.

Loving the feel of his skin, Suzanne stroked his shoulders and arms, then trailed the pads of her fingertips lightly against his chest. She breathed in unison with him, her breathing as shallow as his. She reveled in the feel of him, of his own erotic touch on her body.

Responding in kind, she mimicked his every move so that each was a mirror image of the other.

He brushed her mouth with his. She parted her lips, hoping, praying he would press further. But he didn't. Smiling, he taunted her again and again.

Suzanne leaned toward him, bracing her hands tightly against his waist. Still he refused to deepen the kiss.

"David," she murmured. "Please."

"I love the way you sound when you want me," he whispered hoarsely. "Say my name again."

"David. David. David," she repeated.

He covered her mouth with his, commanding a kiss from her that would never be forgotten. Arms entwined, they stood in the moonlight and exchanged the silent words of love and worship conveyed by touch and whisper.

With hands that shook, David led her to the bed and lay down with her. Lying by her side, he watched her face, demanding her excited gasps, her sighs with his touch.

Every stroke healed a small emotional wound. Every touch promised more. The tension built to an unbearable pitch, and Suzanne heard her voice echo David's into ecstasy.

5

DAVID STARED through the skylight at the stars blanketing the night. Suzanne was asleep, her head resting on his chest. Her small hand curled around his neck, as if she didn't want to let him go. He loved the feeling. When he tightened his embrace, she snuggled even closer.

He wanted to shout with pleasure and love. Exclaim his happiness from the mountaintop. Hug her tighter. Dance around the room with her in his arms. He'd found her again, and this time she would remain his.

But he couldn't do it. At least not right now. Who knew what the future held? He'd done things this past week that he would have sworn neither he nor Suzanne was capable of doing. All through his married life with Barbara, he'd never cheated on his wife. He'd never expected to cuckold another man, either, but he'd just made love to a married woman.

Just thinking about it should have made him feel guilty. With anyone else he probably would have. But not with Suzanne. In his mind, Suzanne had been his for so many years that he had a hard time believing that she wasn't his now. He couldn't imagine her with another man, much less a husband. And he wasn't going to try to do so now.

Soon they would have to sort through this mess and figure a way out. The obvious first step was for her to get a divorce. It would take time and it meant separation, but they would do what was needed so they could be permanently together.

Then Suzanne would become his wife. Just as she should have been years ago if tragedy hadn't intervened.

He closed his eyes and sighed. The past was done with. They had children from their marriages, and no one could say that was a mistake. A new life lay before them. Together. It was never too late.

It was too late. Suzanne watched the stars fade from the heaven and light slowly seep into the cloudy sky. Life's twists of fate had insured she could never be with David for longer than this vacation. Tears filmed her eyes, but she fought them back.

Dawn would always come first. After this vacation, Suzanne would disappear from David's life and all this would be a memory. She'd never tell her daughter about her real father. Never. She and Dawn had already tested the limits of their relationship. She wouldn't endanger it any further.

Suzanne remembered with heart-stopping clarity the night that Dawn had run away. She was almost sixteen and had decided that she could come and go when she pleased. Suzanne had set down a curfew. Dawn screamed that it was unfair to change the rules now. Once stated, she believed her mother had to live with what she'd said before. Then Dawn stormed out the door. She never returned that night, although Suzanne waited up until morning, alternately crying, praying and cursing. Late the next night, the police had brought her back, kicking and screaming. Frightened by her life on the streets Dawn had remained living at home.

Now that all the terrible times were behind them, they had finally reached the point where they could really talk to each other. Suzanne wouldn't give that up. *Couldn't* give it up. It didn't make sense to point out that they'd been living a lie. And since Dawn didn't even know there was a real father to discuss, the issue would never come up. Everyone would be safe.

Happiness with David was a fleeting experience, after all. And it would have to remain that way. This time the tears won, streaking her cheeks with wetness. She snuggled closer to David's sleeping form. She would laugh and love and enjoy her limited time with him. She deserved that much. More than that, she would need the memory of these magic moments if she was to go back to New Orleans and live the rest of her life without the man she loved.

David sighed and rolled toward her, pulling her into the comfort of his hard body. His arms wrapped around her and tightened. She sighed and closed her eyes, not really wanting to go back to sleep, but needing to add this time with him to her memory bank—something to cherish for the rest of her life....

THE ROOFTOP WAS PERFECT for a leisurely breakfast. After making love in the early morning, Suzanne had thrown on a gauzy pink sundress, made coffee and a stack of cinnamon toast. Then they ate on the roof, where she could see the rest of the village, the vineyards and the deep blue sea and feel the morning sunlight that poured over them like warm, liquid gold.

"More coffee?" Suzanne asked as she lifted the pot and poured a warm-up into her thick, white mug.

"I'm fine," David murmured, his eyes closed as he leaned back and let the sun wash over him. "Mmm. I think I just found heaven."

"Thanks," Suzanne teased, earning a glimmer of a dimple in his unshaven cheek.

His hand rested on her thigh. "Sitting in the Italian sun with you is like heaven."

"A likely story." His words tinted her skin to the tone of a ripened peach she knew. She hadn't been complimented in a long time and it felt great. If this wasn't a part of her fantasy, she didn't know what was.

"Annie?" David's voice was light, yet distant. His eyes were still closed, his manner relaxed.

But Suzanne's nerves went on alert. "Yes?"

"Are you happy in your marriage?"

No. Her mind formed the word instantly. She'd been unhappy for so long. After separating, it had taken a year to understand just how unsuitable she and her husband had been. Now, three years later, she realized that for her, the single life was far better. The divorce proceedings this past spring had only put on paper what she had felt for a long time.

"It's not really a happy marriage," she hedged. He didn't know she was divorced—and he couldn't know.

"Then get out of it now."

"What's *now* got to do with it?"

David opened his eyes and stared at her during a long, uncomfortable moment before answering. "Doesn't it seem odd that you're married to one man while you're making love to another?"

She wanted to defend herself, but couldn't, and that was frustrating. "If you're attacking my morals," she retorted, her anger barely leashed, "doesn't it seem odd to you, upstanding and moral man that you are, that you just made love to a married woman? Or doesn't that bother you?"

All her instincts told her to end this affair and walk away from him. But part of her still ached to fulfill her own fantasy. After all, she reasoned, how many times did people get to relive their past and find it as delicious as the daydreams?

"Making love to a married woman isn't quite the same thing that you've been doing, and you know it."

Judgmental, too. She was glad she had to let him sweat—even if just a little—about their "sins."

"No, I don't. So don't be too quick to condemn. You don't know anything about me."

"Don't I make a difference in your life?" he growled, anger and frustration replacing his earlier patience.

"Why, because *you're* free?"

"Yes." He dared her to deny it.

But she knew about Dawn, and he didn't. Suzanne couldn't take the chance that Dawn might never forgive her. Maybe what she was doing wasn't right, but she didn't have much choice.

She looked away, over the rooftops and through the TV antennae to the sea beyond. Her gaze didn't capture the beauty. Instead she saw the empty loneliness of her life ahead. She shook off the premonition. What was done was done, and all she had to look forward to was the here and now. Once back home, she would retire again to that other, staid existence.

Her silence hung in the air, making clear her choice.

David's sigh dispelled some of the tension that had accumulated. "Okay, Annie," he said in a tired voice. "Obviously you're spoiling for a fight, but I'm not going to indulge that whim. We'll discuss this another time." He leaned over and took her hands. "But please, start thinking about it now. Because we will discuss it *soon*. We've got less than two weeks together."

Suzanne searched his face. His eyes held a different, stronger message. His determination was etched in the lines around his mouth and the frown on his forehead. But he was willing to choose his timing better. She could see he wasn't secure enough about her to press this moment. That was all right with her, because she didn't ever want to talk about it.

She nodded. "All right. What are we going to do today?"

"We're taking the train farther down the coast, finding a deserted beach and having a picnic."

Suzanne felt her eyes widen. "Did you just think of this?"

His chuckle washed over her like a warm wave. "I've dreamed of this for years. This is the first time I'm implementing my idea, though."

"You never had picnics in Oklahoma?" she teased, unwilling to admit just how much she was relieved at the change of topic.

"No. With Barbara in a wheelchair, she didn't want to bother. Since her death two years ago, Jason and I haven't had time to remedy that." The sadness that was always with him when he spoke of his wife colored his tone. Then he smiled. "Besides, in my imagination all my picnics took place in Italy. With you."

"At eighteen, not forty," she stated wryly.

"At any age," he corrected, his voice turning husky, making her think of other ideas he might have had.

Her body responded even before she could stop herself.

David looked down, his gaze plainly snared by the curve of her breasts through the gauzy material of her sundress. She felt her nipples harden in response and heard him catch his breath, then he stood and held out his hand to her. With a slow but steady motion, she accepted his clasp and walked with him through the door, down the stairs and into the bedroom.

They had problems, but they also had desires. The problems were many and would be worked out later.

Desires, however, were different animals. They could be worked out now. Right now....

TWO TRAIN STOPS south of Vernazza was another medieval village that didn't reach as far as the sea. A quarter-mile walk across black dirt and chunky rocks was rewarded by a silver and black sandy beach with boulders the size of boxcars, making each clear space a miniature, very secluded Eden. Not even the ever-present breeze was rude enough to invade their privacy.

David peeled off his shorts to the bathing trunks underneath. He watched Suzanne do the same, marveling that her slim body, although filled out by maturity, was still so youthful after two children. Oh, there were a few laugh lines around her eyes, a furrow on her forehead that wrinkled becomingly when she teased or frowned at him. But time had only increased her sex appeal. She seemed more subdued and restrained than she'd been in their youth, but occasionally allowed her impish love for life to penetrate the veneer of sophistication. He wanted her to retain that high-spirited joy always—with him.

Suzanne spread the silver blanket on the sand and lay down. Her eyes closed, she reminded him of what she'd looked like this morning when he'd awakened her with his need: sleepy and sensuous and seductive. He felt himself hardening again, wanting the woman he'd loved since he'd been the romantic youth who'd believed he could control the direction of his own life.

Without opening her eyes, Suzanne patted the area next to her. "Aren't you interested in working on that tan?"

"I'm more interested in working on your body."

She smiled, eyes still closed. "Not from there, you aren't."

Her slim hips moved over to allow him enough room and his breath came thick in his throat. How could she affect him this way after all these years? He felt like a teenager again, ready to conquer the world—and the woman he loved.

Stretching out beside her, he balanced himself on his side and lightly stroked her milky skin from ribs to sweetly rounded stomach.

"Mmm." She placed her hand over his. "That tickles."

"Does it really?" he taunted, continuing as lightly as possible, his fingertips barely touching her skin. Her hand tightened on his but didn't stop him.

"Yes," she admitted, her voice dropping several notes. Then she took the initiative, her hand leading David's around her soft curves and warm spots. He allowed her to wander where she might, curious and excited to see what was going to happen next.

She ran his hand from hip to hip, then traced rib to rib, touching one at a time. Then her hand raised his until he stroked her neck and throat, feeling every hollow, every nuance. She halted his travels for a second and he could feel the rapidity of her breathing. He wanted her. He wanted her so badly, he thought he'd die of the exquisite pleasure of waiting.

Still he allowed her to lead. When she hesitated over her right breast, he took over. His hand lightly cupped her soft flesh, his thumb flicking gently over her nipple and watching it pucker through the light, elastic material. The pulse in her throat resembled the beating of a hummingbird's wings against the creamy flesh, as if it were trying to escape.

With a deft movement, he pulled down the bathing-suit and enjoyed the sight of her unveiled breast.

He bent his head. His mouth circled the dark areola before tugging it into his mouth and laving it with his tongue.

David felt her breath stop completely and redoubled his efforts. She was so still, so stiff that he knew she hadn't felt this way in a long, long time.

He gloated. Her marriage was a sham. Her reaction to him confirmed that he'd been right all along. He should have known before this, but last night all he had understood had been his own desire.

When a moan escaped her throat, he lost patience. His hand sought and found the warmth of her, seeking that very essence that made her feminine. Her back arched in response. Suddenly she was moving, touching him, silently asking for his mouth on hers. He obliged, checking his passion as he continued to love her.

Her back arched, her mouth claimed his. "Oh!" was the sound that pleased him most. Then she was shuddering in his arms.

He'd done it. He'd brought her the greatest pleasure without considering his own needs. The feeling of both power and pain was incredible.

His heart thudded heavily against his chest as he soothed her body into a relaxed, subdued state. Her eyes fluttered open, closed, then opened again.

Her hand brushed against his jawline, following the cord down his throat to his heart. "Thank you," she said softly.

He smiled tightly. "You're welcome."

"And now," she said, pushing against his shoulder until he was flat on his back and she was on her side, gazing sexily down at him. "It's my pleasure to pleasure you...."

THEY ATE DINNER at Tina and Arturo's little restaurant, sitting in a far, cozy corner inside the long, narrow building. They'd been out all day and Suzanne wanted both privacy and relaxation.

"Tell me more about your life," she prompted, twirling her spaghetti around a fork. "What's a typical day like?"

David sipped his wine. "I'm not sure anymore," he admitted. "With Jason out of high school and going away to college, twelve years of routine will be gone."

Suzanne understood. She'd suffered through the same experience when Dawn had gone away to college. And this year her baby would be leaving. She'd be alone.

Suzanne cleared her throat, wishing she could clear her thoughts as easily. "Will he be going away to college or staying at home?"

"He wants to stay at home and I want him to go away to college."

"Really? I thought all eighteen-year-olds wanted to go away, have fun and live off their parent's largesse."

"Is that what your daughter is doing?" he asked casually.

"Dawn is going to be a CPA."

Before he could comment, Arturo strolled from the kitchen to their table, wiping his hands on his apron. "It's good, eh?" he asked, not really waiting for an answer. "I do the best fettuccine Alfredo. Everyone says so. Even Tina."

Suzanne laughed. "It's delicious," she admitted. "As usual, Arturo. Thank you for asking."

But he didn't leave. Arturo's eyes focused on the man across from her. "You been here before. Much younger then, eh?"

Suzanne felt a light flush tinge her skin and wondered how she could stop Arturo from revealing too much.

David's hand covered hers protectively. "Yes, I met Suzanne here when I was just out of college and she was out of high school."

"Did you marry?"

"Yes. I have a son who's visiting Saint Tropez right now."

"Saint Tropez, it's nice. But not as nice as Italy, eh?" He got the laugh he wanted, then Arturo stared hard at David. "You don't mean to hurt our Suzanne? You have a family at home, eh?"

"I'm a widower," David explained slowly. "And no. I don't mean to hurt Suzanne."

"Okay, then." He winked at Suzanne, then smiled. "It's good food, eh?"

"Delicious."

"Eat up, there's plenty more," Arturo ordered, then walked back to the kitchen and disappeared.

David smiled. "Is he that protective of all his relatives, or just you?"

Suzanne relaxed. Her secrets were safe, and she could enjoy the moment. "You should see him with his daughters. I pity any male, old or young, who is interested in the Sottosanti girls."

"So do I." David's tone was heartfelt.

Still laughing, they tinkled their glasses together. "Here's to another reason to enjoy adulthood," David announced. "You don't have to account to everyone at every moment."

"Amen," she said before sipping her wine. "There has to be some truth to the adage about growing old gracefully."

He picked up his fork and played with his pasta. "Don't you think people can have a bright outlook when they're older, too?"

"No." Her answer came straight from the heart. "We can try, but it's not the same. Living and being responsible for others takes its toll."

"Sometimes we grow so cautious that we may not allow strangers to become friends."

Suzanne pursed her lips as she remembered some of her so-called friends who, long ago, had found out she was pregnant with Dawn. They had deserted her. There had been no moral support from anyone except her family.

Until John came along. She'd erected a shell around herself and he'd seen someone as solitary as himself, a soul mate. She'd believed she'd found someone who cared for her, faults and all. What she got was something quite different. John was a man who enjoyed pointing out her faults—all for her own good, of course. The longer they were together, the more faults she had.

"Annie?" David's voice finally got through her thoughts to bring her back to the present.

She forced a smile. "I'm sorry. What were you saying?"

He leaned forward. "Are you all right?"

She made her smile wider. "I'm fine," she said. "Honest."

They ate the rest of their meal in silence. Afterward they strolled hand in hand across the piazza and up the steps to the medieval tower terrace.

Standing at the stone wall, they watched night make Vernazza even more picturesque. It was a beautiful view, all satin-black molten lava and moonlight. Across the cove were the dancing lights of another village. The large moon overhead smiled down, benignly bestowing its blessing upon everything touched by its beams.

David clasped his hands at the back of her waist. He stared down at her, eyes warm with an emotion that seductively stroked the very core of her. "Annie, what is it? What was it I said that put you in this pensive mood?"

She was amazed he felt the slight temperament change, awed that he cared enough to ask about it. No one, especially her ex-husband, had ever noticed small things like that before.

Suzanne shook her head, unwilling to think about her failed marriage. The next two weeks were her special time to be happy. It was going to have to last the rest of her life, so she might as well enjoy it now and worry later.

"There's nothing wrong. I get a little melancholy at times, that's all."

David searched her face and she knew he spotted the sadness in her eyes, but there was nothing she could do to prevent that.

He pressed once more. "Are your children okay? Have you heard from them lately?"

"The children are fine." This was her time with David, dammit! And she was going to enjoy it, even if he decided otherwise.

"Come on." She grabbed his hand impulsively and began to scoot over the low stone wall to the rocks and deserted beach below. Every once in a while she looked back to find him studying her, the intensity of his gaze burning her insides and recklessly heating her blood to a boil.

The sound of the water lapping against the rocks and eerily echoing in the caves was the only sound in their world.

When David turned her to face him, she put her fingers softly over his mouth. "Listen," she whispered.

He did. A light spray wet them. A baby bat uttered a tiny, high-pitched squeal. A gurgle came from the small eddy pond to one side as the water ebbed away and returned to the sea.

Her eyes met his. "Don't you love it?" she murmured.

"I love you."

They were both still in the darkness. She couldn't speak. She couldn't find the words to explain how she felt about his declaration. About him. About this moment.

Instead she tried to tell him that with her silence she loved him, but that it would never be more than what they had at that moment. She reached up and touched his jaw with her fingertips, then outlined his lips with a nail.

"Tonight is ours," she said softly. "Tonight we can conquer the moon and stars. Tomorrow will be different."

She stepped away from him, watching his expression. With studied casualness, she reached for the hem of her shirt and pulled it over her head. She unclasped her bra and threw it to join the blouse. Hooking her fingers inside her waistband, she pulled down her loose white slacks and panties, stepping out of them as if she were wearing a suit underneath them.

The thought made her grin. That was exactly what she was wearing—a birthday suit!

"Join me?" she taunted as she turned toward the sea.

David shed his clothing with impatient movements. Suzanne waded out until the cool liquid spilled against her hips, so that her skin sheened with moon drops. She dived cleanly, coming up just feet from where she'd disappeared. Long, supple strokes took her farther from shore.

David watched, mesmerized. She could have been a goddess. She could have been anything, but she was his. His! She was a part of his very soul.

He ran through the shallow water until it reached his waist, then dived in and followed in Suzanne's wake. Swimming strongly, he caught up with her.

Just before he reached her, she dived again and came up behind him. Swinging around he saw her, hair thick and shiny like mink, outlining the perfect shape of her head. Her eyes reflected the moonlight and dazzled him with the image. Her full lips were caught up in a smile that both taunted and tantalized. It was the most blatant, sexy, wonderful smile in the whole wide world.

Most people never got the chance to be twenty-one twice. David wasn't going to waste it.

He dived a second time and found her. Circling her tiny waist with his hands, he came up laughing. So did she.

"You were quicker than I was. That's not fair!" she exclaimed.

"You had your chance," he muttered, drawing her close. Her hands reached around his neck and held on as he dragged her body against his. Their legs entwined. "It was a fair fight. But the better man won."

"Sexist," she murmured before pulling his head down. Her tongue dueled, then captured and tamed his own. Her hand tangled in his hair, tugging him as close as she could get him. Water was slick against their bodies, wrapping them together as the tide eddied around them.

Suzanne rubbed her breasts against the coarse hair on his chest and he moaned. With a sureness born of demand, he carried her out of the water and laid her upon sand that still held the heat of the Mediterranean sun.

He knew his gaze was hot and possessive as she smoothed his damp hair away from his face, her eyes like giant emeralds in a sea of cream. Something deep inside him snapped. Expressing a primitive need, he entered her. Her legs wrapped around his waist as he merged his body with hers.

And when the ecstasy came, they both cried out, too amazed to fight the momentary drowning of their senses.

Even in the afterglow of making love, he felt a sadness. Suzanne looked as if she wanted to say something and he wanted to share her worries. He needed to know what she was thinking. He just didn't have the nerve to ask. . . .

Vernazza

The word love is constantly on the tip of my tongue. I've swallowed it at least a thousand times in one day. At least I can write it once: I love David. I always have, I always will. And making love with him is something that I thought was only written about in books. I feel light and wonderful and sensuous. I've never felt this seductively feminine. I've never felt this alive.

And I know I'll never feel so alone as when he leaves.

6

"MOM?"

Suzanne stood in Tina's living room, holding the phone tightly against her ear. It was so good to hear Dawn's voice! "Hi, Dawn. How are you? Where are you?"

"We're in Venice and it's absolutely the best city in the whole world! Everything's so neat. Even the taxis are motorboats. It's the only way you can get around. It's either that or walking." Dawn stopped for breath, but not long enough for Suzanne to comment. "It reminds me how you described Vernazza. No cars."

Suzanne laughed. "I gather you're having a great time?"

"We're having a ball!" Dawn exclaimed. "Eve got picked up by some scummy guy with a tattoo, but I told her no more than one date, and she had to be back at the hotel before the doors closed at ten."

Suzanne heard Eve moan and grinned. Dawn, ever practical, would not allow impetuous Eve to stray too far from home values. Sometimes Suzanne thought that Eve only thumbed her nose at those common-sense rules because she felt she was supposed to. If she didn't, then Dawn would have nothing to gripe about.

"Is Eve watching you as carefully?"

"Eve's watching anything that moves, but not me. I can take care of myself."

Eve's moan came again, this time with an admonition for her sister to shut her mouth or she'd stuff a sock in it.

Dawn ignored her. "So how's the writing coming, Mom?"

Suzanne had the grace to feel guilty. "I haven't begun to write yet, honey," she admitted.

"I thought that was what this was for!" Dawn exclaimed. "Or have you met some wonderfully dashing Italian count and fallen in love?"

I met your father and I fell in love. Again. "There's a shortage of Italian counts this year. Would you believe that none of them have decided to spend their vacation in Vernazza?"

"Well, they just don't know what they're missing." Dawn obviously felt she was the only one who could talk back to her mother.

"What can I say?" Suzanne said with a laugh. "Now let me speak to your little sister so I can whip her into shape."

"Right. We thought we'd run down to Vernazza and visit you on our way to Florence. You know, sort of a detour."

"No. That's not a good idea. I'll be getting into my work, and you should spend as much time as you can in Florence. It's one of the most wonderful cities in Italy."

"Mom? Are you okay?" Dawn asked. "We were only going to visit for a day or so." She was obviously hurt. "It's your birthday."

"I know, honey. Tell you what, I'll take Tina with me and we'll meet you in Florence. It is *my* birthday and this trip will make it a special celebration. Tina hasn't had a holiday for some time and she could use the change of scenery," Suzanne improvised.

"Are you sure?"

"I'm sure. I owe her the trip anyway because I won a bet. When will you arrive in Florence?"

"A week from Wednesday, since we're not coming to Vernazza."

Suzanne knew Dawn was puzzled by her behavior, but she had to protect her daughter, and that meant keeping her away from David Marshall.

"Wonderful. We'll meet you at your hotel."

"Terrific," Dawn said, sounding mollified. "We'll only call you if plans change, then."

"Great, honey. Now let me talk to the one who's in love with tattoos."

Eve's lilting voice came onto the line and Suzanne chatted with her for a few minutes. After assuring herself once again that they weren't coming anywhere near Vernazza, she hung up.

Tina sat on her couch, her bare feet propped up. Her gaze was steady and all-knowing. "You won a bet?"

Suzanne smiled, but knew it was forced—and knew that Tina knew, too. "Sure I did. I said you would go to Florence with me if Arturo couldn't wait fifteen minutes to come out from the restaurant."

Tina stared at her. "The day you arrived?"

Suzanne nodded.

"You saw him come out as you were leaving?"

Suzanne nodded again. "So you don't have a choice. I won fair and square."

Tina leaned back. "So we're going to Florence to keep the kids away from David."

"You certainly know how to get to the heart of the problem."

"Don't get flippant with me," Tina retorted. "Just the facts, ma'am. Are we or are we not going to Florence so the kids don't meet David Marshall?"

Suzanne took a deep breath. "That's exactly the reason we're going. That, and the fact that I won the bet. Don't be a sore loser, Tina. The family will be able to survive without you for a few days."

Tina was clearly more than a little surprised. "I remember. I remember." She was obviously wishing Suzanne hadn't. "I just didn't think you did."

"I wasn't completely oblivious to what you said, even though I seemed so at the time." Suzanne laughed nervously.

"Then I may use you again as a sounding board. But are you really going to hide Dawn from David forever?"

Every time they were together they rehashed this subject. "Please, Tina. You know I'm going to continue with the way I've chosen."

"Even though it's the wrong way?"

"It's the wrong way for you," Suzanne said. "For me, it's the right way, Tina. Honest."

Tina looked as if she was about to argue, then her shoulders slumped and she gave in. "Okay, okay, but this isn't right. For either of them. Dawn has always wondered about her father, and there's very little I could tell her."

"When did you two discuss this?"

"Two weeks ago, when they were in Milan. Dawn called and I was telling her about the restaurant and she asked if her father had liked to cook. I told her I didn't know."

"Was that it?"

"Yes. But there have been other times when she's asked more questions. She wants to know."

Suzanne became defensive. "If she wants to know more, tell her to talk to me."

"I have." Tina's tone was firm. "She won't. She thinks his death is too painful for you to discuss."

Suzanne tried to sort through her thoughts as she paced the long room. "Maybe if I had told Dawn the truth about her father when she was little, we wouldn't be in this spot now. I don't know. But I never expected to see David. John and I agreed to tell her that her father had died. And she accepted it. We said the same lie so often, we began to believe it." Suzanne stared down at her hands, which were clenched tightly together. With extreme precision she unlocked them. "It's too late to change the past, including the part where Dawn and I hardly talked to each other for weeks on end, unless we were shouting. This is the only thing I ever lied to Dawn about, but it's important. She'll never trust me again."

"But—"

One hand raised in the air, Suzanne interrupted. "Don't you see Dawn has always been so serious. Even when she was on her worst behavior, she was honest. She's so intense. I'm not sure she'd forgive me, and I can't take the chance of losing her. I love her so much, and she might not ever love me again." Her throat closed and she swallowed hard. "I couldn't stand that."

"Of course she'd still love you." The words were an affirmation, but Suzanne heard indecision in Tina's voice.

"I don't know that. Neither do you. I can't take the chance, and I won't have anyone else taking that chance, either. Dawn is still a little girl at heart. She doesn't have any idea just how vulnerable I am to her anger or withdrawal of affection. Until she's old enough to know better, I will not allow anyone to hurt our relationship."

"Okay. You win. I promise I won't say or do anything that will allow her to know the truth. Not because I think it might hurt your relationship with her, because that can always be healed. But because it might hurt you." Tina stood and gave Suzanne a hug. "I don't want you hurt, honey."

Suzanne smiled through her tears. "It'll work out. You'll see." She pulled back. "And you've always loved Florence in the summer...."

LATER THAT AFTERNOON, as Suzanne sat in front of her typewriter and reread her notes, she tried not to allow her thoughts to return to that conversation with Tina.

Stop it! Now that the decision was made again and Tina understood it, she could get back to her writing.

She rolled a fresh sheet of paper into her machine and began typing. Suddenly she was in another world, but one where she had complete control—unlike her own life. Excitement poured through her, her fingers could hardly keep pace with the rush of imagination.

As she typed she could see her characters in front of her; hear their voices, feel the emotions! They became real people—as real to her at this moment as anyone she had ever known.

A knock at the door interrupted her. "Come in!" she shouted.

The door opened, but no one said anything. "What is it?" Suzanne asked, not looking up.

"I'm not sure my timing is right." David's voice brought her back to this world—the real world of David and Dawn, of happiness and sorrow. She swung around.

He stood framed in the doorway, dark and handsome. She shifted uneasily, wishing she could change their past. But she couldn't. She noticed the room was filled with shadows. "What time is it?"

"About six-thirty. We were going on a picnic tonight. Remember?"

Her heart sank. Much as she wanted to be with him, she also wanted to finish this scene. It was going so well.

David's gaze switched quickly to the typewriter, then back to her. "You're in the middle of something, aren't you?"

He turned and picked up the wicker basket that sat at his feet. With a deft movement, he swung it into the room and dropped it next to the couch before sitting down. "Don't worry. I wanted to read an article in this magazine, anyway. Finish your writing."

"But I—"

"It doesn't matter how long it takes. I'm a big boy, I can wait for my dinner. Whenever. No problem." His understanding smile warmed her.

Still reluctant, she turned back to the machine. It should have been awkward to write with someone watching her, but wasn't. She reread the last two sentences and was back inside the story.

She squinted at the sheets, her typing slowing to a stop when she realized there was no more light pouring in from the window. Turning, she was surprised to see David still there—asleep. She tilted her head to see which magazine he'd wanted to read: *Cosmopolitan*—in Italian.

She walked over to the couch and covered his lips with a butterfly-light kiss.

He didn't move, but a light "Mmm," filtered through his lips.

She did it again.

His mouth remained still, but his arms circled her waist and pulled her into his lap. Then he responded, kissing her boldly.

Breathless, Suzanne pulled away. "You're awake."

"I certainly am," he muttered, then covered her mouth with his once more. With a twist she was on her back and David was stretched out beside her, his lips now touching her with the same teasing softness she had used earlier.

"I like this," she whispered.

"So do I." His lips grazed her eyes.

"All this and I get fed, too?"

"You bet. Take your pick."

"Pick?"

He nibbled on her bottom lip. "You can feed on me or the contents of my picnic basket."

She opened her eyes and stared at his mouth. "Both."

"I'm warning you, you could overeat."

Suzanne laughed. "I know, but it's part of the price I pay for being a glutton."

One hand trailed from her breast to her waist, then curved up over her hip. "Hourglass figure," he murmured. "So very nice."

Her hand moved over his shoulder and down his side. "I agree. Very nice."

Then he took her mouth with his and nothing else was said.

It wasn't until much later that they spread the contents of the hamper across the living-room floor. David filled glasses with wine. Fried potatoes sprinkled with a light coating of vinegar were heaped on one square of paper, while strips of fried white fish were dunked in a light, creamy sauce.

David fed her a piece of fish, then watched as she swallowed. "Good?" he asked.

She nodded. Right now, the world felt like one big warm fuzzy.

"Do you have living-room picnics often?" David asked.

She shook her head. Slipping a potato into her mouth, she inquired with a little difficulty, "How about you?"

He nodded. "Of course. All the time. Unlike New Orleans, Oklahoma has snowy winters. Living-room picnics were the solution."

"Lucky family."

"Oh, Jason and I started it when Barbara was in the hospital. Everything was so bad then. Instead of eating fast food, we sat on the living-room floor in the firelight and talked. It was a break from our worries about her."

"It had to be very hard on both of you."

"It's hard to watch someone you love die." His voice didn't ask any sympathy. "But we made it through."

"Do you still miss her?" She wished she could take the question back—she knew the answer.

"I miss talking to her. I miss the light in her eyes when I walk through the door. I miss the three of us being a family. Two just doesn't seem to work as well in the give-and-take of conversation."

"I know. Sometimes neither does three, especially if only one is old enough to be the parent."

David stared at her. "I always imagined you with a large family—at least four children. Why didn't you have any more?"

She couldn't look at him for fear he would recall her slip that there were only three of them. "Things just didn't work out that way."

How could she admit that when Eve was about a year old, John had decided he didn't want any more children? He hadn't known they'd be so messy, so loud, so helpless.

So Suzanne had learned quickly not to bother him about the children. He had made his preference clear with his disappearing act. Dawn came down with the mumps, and John taught a short course in another town. Eve broke her leg and, pleading an overflow of paperwork, he didn't come home until nine or ten o'clock every night, until she no longer needed help getting around. All John had done was discuss childcare theory. It was easy to spout ideas without having to put them into action.

David's hand covered her clenched fist. "Annie. Are you okay?"

She managed a week smile. "I'm fine." He didn't look convinced, so Suzanne decided to change the subject. "Did you like law school? Was it everything you thought it would be?"

"Worse." His boyish grin reminded her of all that she had lost. "With a year off, because of Barbara's accident, it took a lot of effort to get back into the rhythm of school. But I got through."

He picked up another piece of fish and popped it into his mouth. "What do your daughters plan on doing with their lives?"

"Dawn's finished college, and Eve just graduated from high school, like your Jason. Both are independent and feisty and believe they can conquer the world."

"Maybe they can."

She shook her head. "No. As they go through life, they'll discover there are obstacles they won't be able to overcome."

"You sound so cynical about the world."

"It's the only one we've got, so it really doesn't matter whether or not I like it."

"You said that Dawn was like her father. What is your husband like?"

He didn't know those were two different questions. "She's tall and slim, with brown hair and blue eyes. She's much quieter than her younger sister, but if her temper flares, watch out. She's lethal."

David's low laugh touched her deep inside. Sitting on the floor in a rented apartment, discussing their daughter, was both strange and wonderful. It was exhilarating to talk about her with the man who—if he knew—would care as much as she did.

"What is Eve like?"

Suzanne laughed. "Oh, she's far more self-confident, a little boy crazy, funny and mischievous. She looks a lot like me, but acts like no one in the family. My mother used to say she reminded her of me, because when I was young I was so impetuous, but that stopped when—when I became a mother."

David reached for another fry. "Did motherhood change you that much?"

"More than you know."

"In what way?"

How could she tell him that it was the devastation of being rejected by the man she'd loved? And having to go through the humiliation of carrying a child out of wedlock in a society that condemned such behavior?

"The responsibility. The work." She smiled without feeling it inside. "But I'm not as heavyhearted as I used to be."

He brushed a strand of hair from her cheek. She gazed into his eyes and was suddenly eighteen years old again. Lighthearted and impetuous. "I guess you know you're so handsome it makes my teeth hurt," she murmured.

"I never heard that before. But if my looks please you, I'm glad God made me this way."

"So am I."

The teasing look left his face. "Annie, what are we going to do?"

She couldn't pretend she didn't know what he was talking about. She tilted her chin defiantly. "Nothing."

His blue eyes flared with anger. "Are we going to continue with this arrangement until it's time to leave? Then what?" He leaned toward her. "Am I supposed to forget what's been happening between us? Is that it?"

His accusations hurt, but she smiled sweetly in spite of her outrage. "Why not? You did that very same thing the last time we were here." Her gaze skimmed his jean-clad legs and bare chest. "You don't look too much the worse for wear."

David leaned back as if he'd been slapped. "That's a low blow, Annie. I didn't expect that from you."

"Really? Perhaps it's because you don't know me at all."

"Perhaps I don't. But I thought I knew that Annie very well, all those years ago."

It was her turn to be angry. "No, and that Annie got hurt. She was so dumb and so damn naive, she didn't think anyone would purposely set out to hurt her. But she was wrong."

"I was hurting, too, Annie."

"You knew I'd be devastated at not hearing from you. And you knew why you couldn't come to me. But you never thought to share those facts with me."

"Oh, I thought about it. I just couldn't do it. I couldn't talk about what I was going through, and I don't think you would have realized or understood the problems. You were so very young, Annie."

"It wasn't your choice to decide what I was capable of understanding," she said sadly. "It should have been mine."

"I was trying to protect you."

"You didn't have that right."

"I thought I did."

Suzanne shook her head. "I learned the hard way that men don't say what they mean or carry through with their promises. All they do is pretend to be or do whatever it takes in order to get what they want. That youthful Annie was a victim. I'm not."

"That's cruel," he began.

"And congratulations, David Marshall," she continued, ignoring his accusation in favor of one of her own. "You were the first to teach me about empty promises." She stood up and glared at him. Memories of those traumatic months flashed through her mind. If David had at least contacted her, she might have had an easier time of it. At least she might have understood.

"I'm asking you to forgive me, Annie, so we can get on with our lives. Together."

She clenched her hands to keep them from shaking. "No. Find yourself another woman and see if she wants to believe your sweet-talking words."

"Isn't it time we began again? This is all old stuff now, Annie."

"Because of the way you behaved in the past, we don't have a future. We don't even have a present anymore. I want you out of here in half an hour." Suzanne walked out the apartment door and down the steps. She ignored David's angry shouts. When she reached the dark piazza, Suzanne broke into a run, taking the only street up the side of the hill, under the train bridge and on. She ran until it hurt to draw breath.

Then, forty-year-old Suzanne Lane sat down on the black earth and cried for what might have been.

Vernazza

I thought I knew him, and once more I let my day-dreams go too far. Damn the man! I never should have taken up with him again. It's all his fault that I spent the better part of my life feeling so very lonely.

    I hope I never see him again!

    But I already miss him.

7

DARKNESS WAS COMFORTING. Suzanne stared up at the night sky. The stars that she had wished upon when she first met David were now a bitter reminder of unfulfilled dreams.

What had she done? By getting involved with David again she was welcoming heartache. And she had put her daughter in a vulnerable position. How could she have done that to her child—and herself? Others called her practical and down-to-earth. Granted, she hadn't been that way as a young woman; she had learned the hard way to plan out every move, to avoid making a bad choice.

Yet now she'd just made the worst choice she could have possibly made. David was a great lover, but had the power to destroy both her life and her own hard-won self-image.

She simply didn't know if she had the strength to change the course their paths had taken. She was honest enough to admit that she would only have the self-restraint to end their affair if he didn't try to convince her otherwise.

When she heard footsteps, she knew immediately who it was. How she wished he hadn't followed her— that he had never returned to Vernazza!

DAVID WAS SO RELIEVED to see her, he didn't know whether to shout in joy or yell in anger. Didn't she realize this was a foreign country? All kinds of things could happen here, as well as at home!

But her expression halted his words. Deciding it was best to say nothing until he figured out what to say, he sat down. His legs stretched out beside hers, as if the two of them were riding a sled, and his arms circled her waist. Calm now that he had Annie in his arms, he rested his forehead on her shoulder. The scent of her was more provocative and intoxicating than the wine made on this hillside. He could feel her heart beating heavily against her ribs, hear her light and shallow breathing. She was alive and vibrant and wonderful. She was as fragile as a bird, as light as air, as tenacious as her hold on his heart.

"I love you."

She shook her head. "Don't."

Still he couldn't let it go. "It's true."

Her heartbeat accelerated beneath his hand. "You don't even know what love is."

"Believe me, I do. You'll probably never understand how much."

"Really? Try me." It was a gauntlet for battle he refused to accept. Suzanne was clearly looking for a fight—for a reason—to end their relationship.

"I'm here now, Suzanne," he said softly, touching her hair with his breath. "I never thought I'd stick around after I found out the woman I loved was married. But here I am. Because I don't want to do anything without you."

"Thanks for sacrificing your noble standards, but I didn't ask you for this." Her voice was as dry and brittle as autumn leaves. Her body was so tense he thought it would snap if she moved.

"I know." He tightened his grip, his hand following the soft roundness of her stomach. He wished he could lay his head upon her lap and close his eyes, blocking out everything but Annie and the night's summer breeze. "I didn't ask for it, either."

Their anger died in the silence between them. Slowly Annie's body relaxed against his. He eased his clasp, loosening his hold. She wasn't going to jump up and run away. And if she decided to, what could he do? She was a free woman.

Not quite. She was a married woman, and he was having an affair with her. But she'd been his in his fantasies for so long, nothing else mattered.

Suzanne rested her hand on top of his. Did it signal peace? Eyes closed, he breathed in the scent of her, then barely grazed her temple with a kiss.

The most important thing was that she was here now. He wouldn't ask for more—yet. But he wanted much more. Whatever Suzanne's reservations were he'd get past them. All he needed was time.

"Let's go to bed." He heard the defeat in her voice even as he hung on to hope.

"It will work out," he said firmly. "I don't know how, but it will."

"Don't count on it, David."

"Anything's possible." He stated it with as much bravado as he could.

Annie stared up at him. "Wasn't it possible for you to come to me a year after we met?"

"That was different."

"No it wasn't," she said sadly, her eyes meeting his. "It's just as impossible for me to come to you twenty-two years later."

She was wrong. She had to be. "Why?"

Again Suzanne shook her head. "It doesn't matter why. What matters is that we have until next week together. After that, we won't ever see each other again." She stroked his cheek and he kissed her palm. "All I can give you is this week—take it or leave it."

"You're not leaving any room for compromise."

"This isn't a board meeting. This is my life. Either accept my terms or forget we ever met on this trip."

His breath grew unsteady as the realization hit him—he was going to lose her—now or next week, it didn't matter when. And he didn't know why.

But his choice was clear. "I accept."

IN JUST FIVE SHORT YEARS, Florence's leather shops had increased from twenty to more than several hundred. Hawkers stood in the streets, handing out flyers to lure buyers with claims their store had the best buys in the city.

"Just what every middle-aged woman wants to be reminded of," Tina commented as she eyed a tight, black leather suit in a window. "I might get one thigh into that outfit."

Suzanne laughed. "Don't worry, Tina. I couldn't get into it, either. And I doubt if even Dawn or Eve could." She bent forward and tried to read the tag. "Maybe Theresa could wear it."

Tina looked at her cousin in mock outrage. "What? And give up her wardrobe full of T-shirts with the logos of various cities around the world? Never!"

"You're right. How could I have been so callous? Perhaps I ought to buy it for my mother. She's thinner than you or me."

"What do they say?" Tina asked. "You can never be too thin or too rich?"

"Or too happy. Ask me."

They strolled the length of the fashionable street. Dawn and Eve were due to arrive at their hotel in Florence in an hour or so. Until then, the two mothers were going to enjoy Tina's minivacation.

"Suzanne," Tina began again, her tone thoughtful. "How did your mother react to your divorce?"

"She was glad John and I weren't together anymore. She considered him a gentle but insatiable mosquito—I believe those were her words. He was sucking the life out of me, but it was so subtle all I felt was a small itch."

Tina's smile was smug.

"And I said there is no one who can kill you that way unless you want to be killed."

"That's not true, and we both know it. I think malaria comes from the bite of a tsetse fly."

"Tina." Suzanne's voice expressed a warning.

"Never mind. I was just curious about what Aunt Julia's reaction to David would be."

"It doesn't matter." Suzanne made her voice as firm as her resolve. "When I leave here, I'll never see him again."

"Isn't that a little drastic? You two love each other, or I wouldn't see the long, languid looks and sweet smiles and all that touching going on. It's more than an affair."

"Aren't you the one who called him a big bad wolf?"

Tina had the grace to look embarrassed. "Yes, but that was before we renewed our acquaintance. Besides, Arturo really likes him, and he's got a sixth sense about those things."

"It's supposed to be the woman who has a sixth sense." Suzanne stalled for time.

"Well in this case it's the man," Tina declared emphatically. "And Arturo says that David loves you with all his heart and soul."

"It doesn't matter," Suzanne responded. "I can't pay the price for him to be a part of my life. Dawn is my daughter. She comes first. Always."

"Do they have to know they're related?" Tina asked hopefully, but clearly knew the answer before Suzanne stated it.

"It wouldn't take a genius to figure that out. Her birthday would give it away, to say nothing of the fact that Dawn looks like a carbon copy of her father." Suzanne stared at her cousin.

If Dawn ever realized her father had been alive all these years and that her mother had never told the truth, the damage would be irreparable. True, Dawn was grown and the friction between the two of them had finally eased, but a lie like that would break her trust in her mother forever. Suzanne knew she couldn't face that. Dawn could effectively cut her mother out of her life for such a sin, and Suzanne would be lucky if she ever saw her again.

So she had a week with him before they went back to their own established lives. There was no other way.

Suzanne and Tina reached the hotel and walked through the lobby to the dimly lighted bar at the far end. The air conditioning felt delightfully cool and dry. It still surprised Suzanne how many places in Europe got along without air conditioning. No one could survive a hot and muggy New Orleans summer without it.

Tina sank into a wing chair and sighed. When their waiter delivered the requested drink, she exclaimed her approval. "Ahh, shades of home!"

"Which home?" Suzanne looked doubtfully at her glass. These three ice cubes were melting quickly.

"America. The U. S. of A."

Suzanne looked around. The bar looked European to her. "What are you talking about?"

Tina opened her eyes in surprise. "Why this, of course. We're sipping tea in tall glasses filled with ice. You usually don't find that in Europe."

"I still haven't found it." Suzanne stared into her glass. Three small slivers vaguely resembling cubes floated in her ice tea. "I guess I'm used to a little more ice."

"You Americans," Tina scoffed, instantly switching her allegiance. "You overdo freezing your drinks and heating your food. Everything should be in moderation."

Suzanne sipped her drink. Tina was right. Everything should be in moderation—including her obsession with David. Especially her obsession with David.

She could feel her mood slipping. A shout of greeting from across the room instantly revived her spirits.

"Mom!" the girls called in unison, and Suzanne waved. After hugs and kisses, sodas were ordered. Suzanne took a good look at her daughters. "Eve, you've lost weight."

Eve grinned. "I know! Isn't that wonderful? And I'm eating pasta with every meal! It's the walking that's doing it. Dawn's got me walking so much, the pounds are dripping off."

"Don't overdo it. You're already slim."

"Don't worry, Mom," Dawn said. "Think of her weight as being held at customs. Once she's back home and not walking, it will all return."

Eve's usually girlish figure looked more like a boy's. "I hope you're right," Suzanne finally said.

Suzanne and Tina sat back and let the girls take center stage, telling amusing stories about their experiences in train stations, taxis, tours and hotels. Relieved that there were only three more weeks before both girls returned home, Suzanne decided to enjoy the stories, some of which sounded rather exaggerated—she hoped.

But pride in her daughters overcame her worries. They were beautiful young girls, different from each other, yet close enough to enjoy their differences.

Her attention was caught by Dawn's words. "And then Dad said we could spend an extra hundred because he paid it on our charge card as a birthday surprise for Eve."

"When did you speak to him?" Suzanne asked, earning a look that said she had already been told and obviously hadn't been listening.

"Last night. And he also told us—" Eve stopped, got a nod from Dawn, then continued "—he's getting married."

Suzanne nodded. "I know. He told me before I left that he was thinking about it."

Eve leaned forward. "Have you met her? Is she nice?"

"From what I understand, she's very nice. I believe you both met her at a faculty party last year. She's a secretary at the university and enjoys many of the same things your dad does."

It seemed odd discussing a woman who was about to marry the man she'd lived with for most of her adult life, but it didn't hurt. It was as if some other woman had lived that life with John. Not Suzanne. Not *this* Suzanne.

"Well, I don't care who she is or how much she's got in common with Dad. She's not you, Mom." Suzanne knew Eve was plainly feeling a tug of loyalty and wasn't sure how to react. This was exactly one of the reasons she and John had agreed to share information about their plans: it made it easier on the children.

"Of course she's not. But that doesn't mean you can't like her for herself."

"Really?" Eve asked. "I don't remember meeting her, but you have?"

Suzanne nodded. "A long time ago."

"And you liked her?"

Suzanne nodded again, stretching the truth just a touch. "From what I saw, she was just right for your dad. If I were you, I'd wish him luck and be happy for them. It's time both of us got on with our lives."

The girls stared at her, while she waited for them to absorb these new ideas. She didn't blame them for being nervous about their father's upcoming wedding. It had taken her time to get used to the idea herself. After all, in some ways it still seemed as if some small part of them were attached. It was normal; after all, they'd spent seventeen years together. They shared a history.

She heard of his activities through the girls, the same way he heard about hers. She was lucky—and so were the girls—that he cared enough to think of how his actions would affect his children.

Eve grinned. "And have you found someone, too, Mom? Is that why you're taking Dad's marriage so well?"

David's strong, gentle face came to mind and she knew a blush stole over her cheeks. "Not at all. It's common knowledge that men always marry more quickly after a divorce. And since your father and I discussed it, I've had plenty of time to adjust."

"Mom?" Dawn's face showed concern and Suzanne knew that whatever Eve might miss, Dawn surely would not.

"I'm fine, really." Her reassurances came from the heart. It was Eve's question about marriage for her that she had reacted to, not her ex-husband's new marriage.

They spent the rest of the evening in the hotel restaurant, dining European style—leisurely and with several light courses. No one course would fill up a person, but each tempted the palate for the one following.

That night, after Suzanne climbed into bed, she stared at the ceiling and wondered if this was the feeling she was going to carry around for the rest of her life.

She felt as if a part deep inside her was hollow, unfilled and knew she was lonely for someone to share her life with. Now, she realized she'd felt that way even while married to John.

David Marshall had made her all too aware of who she was lonely for. It wasn't fair. She'd come to terms with her life and was prepared to spend the rest of it alone. She had even begun to like the idea of "doing her own thing," as her kids called it.

But the hollow spot had grown. Since David had made her aware of it again, he'd also chiseled away at the void, enlarging it until it was almost as big as she was. If it grew any larger, she'd fall into it and be consumed. Tonight, as she'd watched her girls, she'd realized just how little they needed her anymore. She'd have their friendship, but it wouldn't be enough to sustain her over the years. And to ask more than that of them would not be fair, either.

What should she do?

There was no answer. It didn't matter. She already knew it. Her heart and the large, growing hollow spot called out for David.

But logic said no—and logic was what ruled her heart and mind now. Logic was all she could trust.

HE MISSED ANNIE as much as Arturo, in fine operatic form, missed Tina. Arturo moped around the restaurant, sighing and clutching his heart in mock despair. Still David found his comic antics comforting, if after twenty-two years Arturo could still feel that way. Love was grand—when it was returned.

Did Annie miss him, too? Or would she walk away from him unscarred?

Would the rest of his life be this lonely? If Suzanne didn't leave her husband and marry him, it would be.

For David Marshall there was no one else.

Florence

After spending a week with David, I look into our daughter's eyes and see him. It's amazing how much they are alike. Her every word and action is his.

This decision gets tougher and tougher to accept. But what choice do I have?

8

BY THE TIME Suzanne and Tina stepped off the train, darkness had descended. Low, dark clouds scudded across the sky and toward the shore. A downpour was predicted.

Suzanne followed Tina as they walked quickly down the hill and toward the piazza. It was dinnertime, but the restaurant wouldn't be very busy because no one would be occupying the outside tables. The interior seated only twenty people.

With a jagged bolt of lightning to announce its arrival, the downpour began just as they reached the restaurant door. Laughing, they entered the reception area.

Suzanne's gaze caught David's immediately. He was sitting at the bar, and his boyish smile warmed her more than the best heated brandy.

He stood, taking the small suitcase from her hand. "I'm glad you're home."

"Glad to be back." Although it had been wonderful to see the girls, she'd missed David. There was so little time.

"So you're back," Arturo declared with gusto. He held a large tray in his hands, but leaned over and gave his tiny wife a kiss on the cheek. "Help out behind the bar, will you? Giuseppe got a fishhook caught in his hand and his wife won't let him work tonight."

"I thought he knew better than that."

"He does, he does, but he was teaching his son the finer points, and the boy got excited. It took twelve stitches." Arturo's voice grew louder as he walked away. By the time he was across the room, the whole restaurant could hear him. "But his wife, she babies him, so who am I to say no?"

"That man," Tina complained, but the smile on her face belied her words. "You're always babied, Arturo." The crowd laughed and Arturo grinned.

Vittorio stood behind the bar. With a flourish he handed Suzanne a glass of wine. "Compliments of a man who admires beautiful women," he said, his teasing tone and appreciative eye telling Suzanne he'd legitimately earned his reputation as a Romeo.

"Thank you, Vittorio. I appreciate the compliment." Suzanne sat down on the wooden stool next to David. "And you, kind sir, are you also admiring beautiful women?"

He nodded, his blue eyes twinkling. "Yes. And there are so many here. But you're definitely my type."

She couldn't help the smile. Tonight, because of the bad weather, there were only a few locals. Most of the women were in their late fifties and early sixties. All of them looked as if they had lived on a steady diet of pasta and pizza.

"You're only saying that because you're a lech."

"Probably," he agreed.

"An old lech at that."

He nodded solemnly, still agreeing. "My biggest problem is that I lust after just one woman."

"Really?" she asked. "Anyone I know?"

"A young woman, much younger than I could hope to be."

"There aren't any. You're younger in attitude than anyone I know."

"I used to be, but when the lady of my dreams left my life, I aged."

"I'm so sorry. Is there any way that lady in question can help?"

"Yes, but it's a new method. Aggressive medicine. She'd have to put herself at my disposal for several hours."

She sipped the wine, but her heart was beating as if she'd run an uphill mountain mile. "Are you sure of the diagnosis and treatment?"

"I'm certain. In fact, the same remedy is good for chills and fever." One long finger touched her cheek, then followed the soft line of her mouth. "Just being near you gives me chills and fever." His voice was low and deep and thick, honey sweet. He touched her chin, then ran a finger down to the dip in her throat.

She swallowed hard. Where was that resolve she'd thought she had? "Maybe you're susceptible to colds."

"No. There are no other symptoms. You're my problem, Annie. You always have been."

Vittorio put a plate of ravioli in front of them, carefully placing a fork on either side of the plate and nodding with satisfaction. "Mama said eat," he told them complacently as he watched their byplay with obvious interest.

"Thank you." David's voice sounded slightly dry, and Suzanne couldn't help but smile. David didn't like being watched.

But she forgot everything as he cut into a plump ravioli and brought it to her mouth. She'd never had a lover feed her. John wasn't the type to do something this sensuous—or this male. The action made her feel treasured and cared for and very, very feminine.

Too much. She wanted him much too much. She wanted him to be a part of her, wanted to touch him, to feel safe and loved and treasured and cherished. She wanted a future with David.

"Your smile is more wonderful than the Mona Lisa's," David said, his voice too low for anyone else to hear.

"Your touch reaches way down inside me."

"I need to hold you."

Suzanne was shocked by how strongly she reacted to those simple words. "No." She wasn't sure what she was protesting. Did he want to make love to her or just hold her? The distinction was suddenly more important than anything she'd ever known.

"Yes." His tone was hypnotizing. "Just hold you against me and listen to the night sounds." He leaned closer and his voice enveloped her like a warm fog. "I dreamed of doing that again. More nights than I can talk about were spent reliving our solitary times at the castle keep."

"Dear sweet heaven," she breathed. Heat invaded every corner of her body. She took a deep breath and wished for more restraint.

The Suzanne she'd been for so long should have found control. But this side of her, the side that had been repressed for so many years, was dying to break out. Now that vibrant, unrestrained side of her personality took charge.

"Let's go up to the castle."

"It's raining." As if to emphasize his point, thunder rolled heavily across the sky.

"We'll change into bathing suits."

His grin was slow in coming, but it made her glow as much as a roaring fire. He nodded toward her glass of wine. "Finish your drink."

"I don't need to."

Tina called as they went into the rain. "Be careful! Don't get struck by lightning!"

David grabbed her hand and they ran across the piazza. A giggle escaped her throat, floating on the damp night air. Her laughter was joined by David's deep tones.

When they made it to the other side of the square, Suzanne caught her breath.

"Kids have all the fun playing in the rain!" David exclaimed. "I wasn't allowed to do it even when I was a kid. Were you?"

"No, but I did it anyway." She plucked the wet blouse material away from her breasts. But the moment she let go of the fabric, it molded itself to her softness.

The laughter went out of David's eyes. With strained movements, he repeated her actions and watched the material glue itself to her body.

Suzanne couldn't move, couldn't breathe as she watched one expression chase another across his face. The rain pelted the cobblestones, lightning momentarily slashing the darkness. "I want you so much I'm shaking."

"You're shaking because you're wet."

"Dry me."

His gaze focused on her mouth. She parted her lips, needing his kiss. But just in case, she leaned toward him and nipped gently at his jaw. A moan escaped him. Then he pulled her into his arms and crushed her against him. Her palms cupped his head, her mouth claiming as much of him as he did of her.

Then he broke away and stared down at her. "Say you love me." His voice was hard with demand. "Say it!"

A lightning bolt hit the sea. "I love you!" she screamed as the thunder rolled over the water to envelop them in sound. "I love you," she whispered in the silence when the thunder stopped.

David's shout of joy echoed off the surrounding walls. "I knew it! I knew it!" He took her hand and reached for the suitcase. "Come on."

Once inside his apartment, she could see that the glow in David's eyes was hot enough to steam her clothing. "You're soaking."

"So are you."

He took a deep breath and pulled wide, linen cloths out of the small closet. "Get undressed and wrap yourself in one of these."

Suzanne undressed with quick movements, threw her clothing across a dining-table chair and wrapped the cloth toga fashion around her body and tied it in a knot.

When she turned, she found David staring at her. He was wearing his cloth tied low around the hips.

Her eyes darted up to his.

David held out his hand. "Let's climb to the roof."

The door at the top of the stairs was slightly open. He pushed at it and it swung back against the building, exposing a long overhang that shielded them from the thick rain pelting down. The night sky seemed immense and the white-capped sea angry. As if performing for their benefit, lightning arched across the sky in a zigzag dance of energy.

Leaning against the stucco exterior, David drew her into his arms, her back toward him. Circling her waist with his arms, resting one hand on her abdomen, he murmured into her ear. "I've been wanting to do this for two days."

"Watch a storm?" she teased, but her heart acknowledged a contentment that only came from being close to, from loving this man. She'd had to wait until she was forty to know this feeling. And now that she knew it, she was going to lose it. . . .

"You know, I needed this." She had to be honest. If not with him, at least with herself. "I needed this more than I knew."

"We both did."

This moment with David was time out of time. She knew it as well as she knew dreams weren't meant to be lived—just imagined. Life had taught her that at an early age. The grander the dream, the harder the acceptance of reality.

"David," she began, afraid that he would spin still more dreams to tempt her. She couldn't take that. She was too tired of fighting life's battles to risk believing in happiness, only to find nothing. Again.

His fingers over her lips stopped her. "Shh," he crooned in her ear. "Lean back and enjoy God's fireworks, Annie. We've got the rest of our lives to work out the details. Let's just enjoy this moment now."

She did as he asked, wanting peace as much as he did. But the details wouldn't be worked out. Not now, not later. This small time was all she had. She might as well enjoy it.

SLEEP WAS FITFUL. Suzanne turned and tossed most of the night, waking up to find David's hands at her waist, arms around her, or snuggled to her back, spoon fashion. She would relax and fall back asleep, only to be wakened by dreams again.

She was living a dangerous life. Her heart and spirit told her that she craved to be with David. But everything she'd worked for, was proud of, needed, would be destroyed if she lost her daughter's love now. She couldn't handle that. It was the reality her life was based on.

She didn't know what to do.

Dawn had come by the time she finally accepted her earlier decision to enjoy this next week, but nothing more. When it was over, she would disappear from David's life. It was the only safe answer.

DAVID FELT Annie's restlessness throughout the night. Something was disturbing her and she didn't want his help. He became aware that she'd been worried about something ever since they'd met, but the only answer he could come up with was her marriage. Obviously she was not happy, or she wouldn't be involved in an affair. It wouldn't matter how much she loved him;

he knew her well enough to know she would never have been tempted if she was happily married. It was his own ego-saving, conscience-salving answer. But he was sure he was right.

The most frustrating part was that he didn't know what he could do to help her deal with her problems and come to a solution that would allow them to be together immediately.

He wanted to help, but she refused to let him into her thoughts. She was so damn frustrating! She wouldn't let him be her knight in shining armor. She wouldn't let him be anything but her lover.

She moaned and rolled over, her hand restless as it caressed his chest. He covered it with his own and she stilled.

They had four more days together, then he had to head back to the States. He decided to give her one month to work out her marital situation. Then he would force her to publicly recognize him as her other half. Because that was what she was to him: his better half. And this time he wasn't going to let time, circumstances or even another man ruin his chance for happiness.

Deep down inside he knew that, although she wouldn't admit it, he was her only chance for happiness.

He just had to prove it to her. . . .

SUZANNE HAD BEEN WRITING for over four hours when little Theresa knocked at the apartment door.

"Mama says Eve is on the phone, and she's calling all the way from Siena!" From the awe in her voice, it was clear Theresa considered this as far away as the moon.

Practically running, Suzanne headed down the stairs and into Tina's home. Tina stood, phone in hand, laughing. "But I don't think your mother will find this as funny as I do, little one," her cousin said as she spied Suzanne. "So you'd better tell her yourself."

Tina smiled as Suzanne arched her brows, then handed over the phone.

"Hi, honey. What's going on?"

"Mom, you're never going to believe this." Eve's voice held laughter and Suzanne began to relax.

"It must be good, because Tina still has a smile on her face."

"Well, yes and no. I fell down and twisted my ankle. It's the size of a balloon right now."

"Have you gone to the doctor?"

"Yes, and he says I have to stay off it for at least a week. And Mom, you should meet this doctor. He's absolutely gorgeous! In fact, he's bringing me dinner tonight. He says I should not be allowed out on my own."

"Oh, really? And did you tell him you were a liberated young woman who can take care of yourself without the help of some macho male?"

"Not for a minute! He's not the type to go for liberation. He's probably never even heard the word. He's the type who wants to take care of a woman."

"Well, let him take care of someone else, honey. You hightail it back here and I'll take care of you."

"But, Mom!" Eve wailed. "He's just a good friend and he *is* a doctor, for goodness sake!"

"He could be Einstein, and I want you here, young lady," Suzanne stated firmly. "You can rejoin your sister in a week or so, when your ankle heals."

"Jeez, Mom, you sound just like Dad," Eve complained. "I expected some enthusiasm from you, at least. Instead I get the same reaction. It's not fair."

"At least your father and I agree on something. Now put Dawn on the phone for me."

Dawn helped Suzanne plan Eve's trip to Vernazza. The train ride was only a little over two hours long, and Eve could sit with her foot up for that length of time. Suzanne had plenty of room in her apartment and Eve could spend her days people watching in the piazza.

It wasn't until the phone conversation was over and Suzanne looked again at Tina that she realized what she'd done.

She sat down. "Oh, my God!"

"I was waiting for you to realize that Eve will meet David. There is no getting around it. Is Dawn coming back, too? Or just Eve?"

"Just Eve, but that's the problem enough," Suzanne muttered, her mind scrambling for an answer to the dilemma. "She's as nosy as a kitten."

Tina sat down with her. "Well, at least it's not Dawn. All she'd have to do is take one look at David and she'd know her roots."

"So might Eve." Suzanne bit her lower lip.

"No." Tina shook her head. "Eve doesn't notice that much about people. She's more into feelings than noticing physical details."

"I hope you're right."

"Just don't make a big deal out of her meeting David, Suzanne. The less she suspects, the better it is. If you try to keep them apart, she'll start wondering what's going on. Then she'll be insatiable until she figures it out."

"You're right." Suzanne put her hands to her head and pressed against the temples. A headache was attempting to get a hold. But she couldn't let it. She had to think this through and figure out how David and Eve could meet without letting him know she was divorced and without letting Eve know that Dawn was David's child.

She had a problem. A big one.

"Only you, Suzanne, could come up with this predicament." Tina's voice was filled with rueful laughter. "It reminds me of our youth. You always got into trouble then, too."

"I've grown up since then, Tina. I don't get in trouble any more."

"Not until now," Tina reminded her. "And I'm sure this will all work out."

"I know it will, too. I just want it to work out in my favor," Suzanne muttered, wondering how this could ever be resolved. She didn't see a way. Fingers crossed, she prayed an answer would pop into her head.

Vernazza

I love David, and in a moment of passion I told him so. How could I have done such a thing? Eve is on her way here and she'll be curious about David. I'm not sure, but I think Eve set me up for this visit. I think she knew that I would insist she recuperate here. Especially once she mentioned the Italian doctor. But why?

Life is so confusing. I thought I was supposed to have all the answers when I got to be this age. Instead, everything becomes even more complicated. I'm so tired of fighting my own happiness, but I don't know what else to do. I keep waiting for an answer— a sign—and all I get are more problems.

9

Eve arrived on the noon train. Suzanne and Tina waited at the station, a child's red wagon at the foot of the stairs in case Eve couldn't manage the downhill slope to the piazza on crutches. But when the bright-eyed girl stepped off the train, she was carrying her crutches and barely hobbling. However, the ankle was bandaged so well, it looked fatter than the average thigh.

"I'm feeling better already!" Eve declared, hugging her mother and favorite second-cousin.

"Your ankle already looks better, we're sure," Tina observed dryly as she picked up the girl's suitcase.

Suzanne caught the innuendo. Eve had come here for more than recuperation. She was up to something. Suzanne or Tina would find out what it was in time.

"It's this wonderful sea air," Eve said, sniffing. "It heals you before you even know you're sick!"

Suzanne watched her daughter barely limp to the stairs and begin the descent. The suspicion she'd been hoodwinked into telling her daughter to return was now becoming a certainty. "And you're a case in point. You've recovered just from a few deep breaths."

Eve didn't look up, but her limp became much more pronounced as she hobbled down the steps, one at a time. "Am I starved! I'm so glad you and Arturo opened that restaurant, Tina."

Even as Eve's questions continued, Suzanne saw her gaze drift from group to group. She had a feeling her daughter was seeking someone, but didn't know whom. Her cousins? They were friends—at least as much as kids can be who are pen pals more than relatives. Each was proud to claim relatives in a far-off land and exchange oddities and examples of higher culture like T-shirts.

Eve perched on the wagon and set her suitcase in her lap. Suzanne began pulling the wagon behind her as Tina walked beside it, asking Eve questions about what she'd seen of Italy so far. She had a remarkable memory, filling the quiet walk back with more information than most people learned in a lifetime.

With each step, Suzanne grew more uneasy. Every motherly sense came screaming to the fore, telling her that Eve was up to something. The second thought was that she wasn't doing whatever it was on her own. Dawn had to be a part of this.

They turned from the main street into the town square and headed toward the restaurant, Eve chatting all the way. Suzanne halted the wagon by a table near the stone wall. After tilting the umbrella so the sun wouldn't be in Eve's eyes, she helped her daughter into a chair and placed another across from her so she could prop up her foot.

Tina took a look at Suzanne's face, then back at Eve, and apparently decided it was time to do something constructive. "I'm going to get us something to eat."

Suzanne pulled up a chair and sat down facing her daughter. She pushed a strand of dark blond hair away from the side of Eve's face. Eve smiled, then glanced down at her lap.

"Do you want to tell me what this is all about?"

Eve's eyes widened. "What are you talking about?"

"Honey, this ankle of yours isn't really bad enough to come here and miss out on vacation unless there's another reason you're here."

"But you *told* me to come here, remember?"

"I understood that your ankle was almost broken and you weren't sure what to do. Apparently, neither was Dawn."

"Right," Eve stated, seeming satisfied that the facts had been correctly stated. "So . . . here I am."

"Doing what?" Suzanne's voice was soft, and she could see her tone worried Eve.

"Mom . . ." Eve began, but never finished. Instead, the smile slipped from her usually happy face, and she frowned at the undulating blue sea.

Suzanne gave her hands a squeeze. "Tell me."

By the way of response Eve closed her eyes, then opened them again. "I got homesick for you."

It might be true. After all, it was Eve's first time to be away from her for so long. And being in a strange country increased the differences. But that wasn't the reason Eve had returned to Vernazza. Not all of it, anyway. Suzanne was certain there was still something else on her daughter's mind.

"And?"

Eve shrugged. "That was it. When I twisted my ankle, it seemed the perfect excuse to see you."

"What about Dawn?"

"Dawn wanted to continue her trek through medieval land."

"And you didn't?"

"I've got the rest of my life to see Europe."

"But you're here now." Suzanne's reminder brought tears to her daughter's eyes.

"Yes." Eve stared at her, and Suzanne sensed the confusion her eighteen-year-old daughter was feeling. "Mom? Are you okay?"

She grinned. "I'm not the one with the broken foot."

"Ankle."

"Whatever."

"No, but you acted kinda funny in Florence."

"Funny? How?"

Eve had the grace to shy away from her mother's gaze. She began twisting the material of her skirt. "I don't know. Like maybe you were hiding something. A secret, maybe. Or something else."

"What a terrific description," Suzanne commented dryly. But her heartbeat picked up a little.

"Well," Eve said defensively. "I wasn't the only one who thought so. So did Dawn. In fact, Dawn thought you and Tina both acted kinda funny."

"And did you discuss why?"

"We thought maybe you found out about Dad."

The hair on the back of her neck tingled. "What now?"

Eve stared at her a moment, dismay apparent in her eyes. Her bottom lip gave a telltale quiver.

"Eve?"

"It's no big deal, Mom," she finally declared. "After all, you didn't want the marriage to go on, either."

Suzanne wasn't about to let her get off so easily. Whatever was bothering Eve was probably also bothering Dawn. "What about your father?"

"He got married last week."

Then she knew. Eve and Dawn both had believed he'd insist on having them with him to celebrate—that although he was remarrying, they were still a part of his life. The shock of realizing that wasn't true had hurt both the girls.

Suzanne reached for her daughter's hands, clasping them in her own. Eve was transparent as glass. "Damn him!"

Eve loosened a hand and wiped away a tear. "Don't be upset, Mom. After all, it's not even our business." Another tear followed the path of the first.

Suzanne's anger instantly disappeared. She gave Eve's hand a squeeze. "It's our business when you feel awkward about talking about it. Don't be so willing to absorb the hurt, honey. Your feelings aren't wrong. Your father should have had the sensitivity to let us all know about his marriage plans. It's only fair to you both."

But her own guilty conscience was already in overdrive. The girls had so many emotions to cope with now. Finding out about Dawn's father would be too traumatic. She heard the final nail hammered into the coffin of her relationship with David. Whatever hopes she had held about continuing with David were killed.

"I knew he was getting married, I just didn't know I'd feel so bad about it, Mom. He could have waited. We'd have been home in a week or so." Eve stopped trying to wipe away the tears. There were too many.

"Honey, he didn't do it to hurt you. In all honesty, your dad probably didn't think. He just did what he wanted to do. Not to shut you out. Not to hurt you—but just because it was what he wanted to do when he wanted to."

"That's all?"

Suzanne nodded. "I'm afraid so. And don't blame Connie, she's a good woman. I'm sure they'll be happy together."

Eve's watery smile turned into a giggle. "Dad says she cooks everything with olive oil and he hates it."

A small part of Suzanne crowed over that remark. The man had criticized her often enough. It only seemed fair that he was now married to a woman who ignored his barbed comments.

When a shadow fell over the table, Eve looked over her mother's shoulder, her breath exiting in a whoosh as she openly appreciated the view. Suzanne knew who it was. There was only one person who would garner such a reaction. One handsome devil.

"Hello, David."

"Hello, Annie. Who's your beautiful companion with the swollen ankle?"

Suzanne saw Eve's eyes light up and inwardly sighed. How could she fault an eighteen-year-old girl for falling for him, when she was forty and her heart did somersaults at the idea of being near David?

"This is my daughter, Eve. Eve, this is David Marshall."

Eve draped her hand casually in front of her so that David was compelled to kiss it. She had expectations of how men in Europe should behave.

Eve's grin broadened, the femme fatale in her clearly trying her wiles on the fascinating older man. "It's nice to meet you, Mr. Marshall. Have you been in Vernazza long?"

"A little over a week. Are you enjoying your trek through Europe?"

"I love it!" Eve enthused. "It's so neat and so *old!*"

"That's Europe for you." He chuckled and she glowed under his gaze. Suzanne knew the feeling.

"What brings you to this little village?" Eve inquired, cocking her head as she studied him. Suzanne felt a chill speed down her spine. Something was bothering her daughter.

"Your mother." At David's simple words, the shiver of apprehension was replaced by fear.

Eve looked confused. "*My* mom?" She looked at her mother, then back up at David.

"*Your* mom," he emphasized. "We met here and became friends years ago, and I came back to see if I could find her again."

Eve's eyes seemed to take up her whole face. "Really?" she asked her mother for confirmation.

Hands now clenched in her lap, Suzanne pretended it was the easiest question in the world to answer. "We met when I was just a kid, and he was finishing up his trip to return to the States and marry his high school sweetheart." She glared at David. "Right?" Her question was a dare.

One that he took as a threat and backed off from. "Right," he answered with a smile. "Your mother was just a kid at the time." He locked eyes with her, his meaning clearly written in his steady blue gaze. "But she was something special, even way back then. So much so that I came here to find out what happened to her."

"Came here? To Tina's?"

He nodded, his attention once more on Eve.

"You know her, too?"

He nodded again. "She had just married your uncle and they were settling into their life here."

"Wow," Eve murmured. "That's so radical."

David grinned again and Suzanne could tell by her daughter's reaction that another woman was under his spell. "It is, isn't it?"

"I mean, it's all so romantic! You came all this way just to find the young woman you remembered in your youth!" she exclaimed. But when she saw the startled look in David's eyes and the laughter in her mother's, Eve backtracked quickly. "I mean, your *young* youth, not that you're not young now. I mean, you could still give Tom Selleck a run for his money. I mean, you're really a terrific-looking guy, even if you were old enough to date twenty-two years ago."

"Thank you for such a nice compliment. In a few years, when I'm really old and gray, I'll remember how a beautiful young woman on the brink of adulthood told me I was handsome."

"You're welcome," Eve said sincerely, in her most adult, feminine voice—about two octaves below her normal speech. She then seemed to recall the gist of the conversation. "Mom? How come you never mentioned him?"

Suzanne felt her face redden and Eve realized her gaffe. "I mean, to me. Obviously others, like Tina and Grandma, knew, but how come you never told Dawn and me?"

Suzanne became nervous again. "There was nothing to tell," she hedged. "Besides, twenty-two years ago I went home, met your father and fell in love."

"Yes, but first you met Dawn's dad, then he died...." Eve's voice faded; she couldn't have failed to see Suzanne's face drain of all color.

David looked closely at Eve. "Died?"

Eve reached for her mother's hand, her entire concentration on the older woman. "Yes, he died in a car crash. Mom met my dad just a few months later."

No, dear God. Not now. Please, not now! Suzanne prayed. She waited for the ax to drop. For David's accusations to be thrown about. For Eve's love to turn to mistrust.

"That must have been doubly hard on your mother." David's voice was comforting.

"Oh, it was tragic," Eve replied, her attention once more diverted. "So very tragic, but then she met my dad and they fell deeply in love." She frowned, and Suzanne saw tears form in her daughter's eyes.

Suzanne's heartbeat stopped. "That's enough. Our family business has been discussed too much already, Eve."

Her daughter's face burned red, but she didn't back off. "But Mom, he's—"

"I said enough." It was an order.

Eve's mouth opened mutinously, then closed.

David smiled at both of them, but Suzanne could read that smile very well. It said: *We'll get to the bottom of this in time, Annie.*

With more courage than she knew she had, Suzanne straightened her shoulders and stared at David. "Don't you think this conversation could wait for another time?"

His eyes narrowed as he studied her. "Perhaps until dinner? Say eight o'clock? Here?"

"I can't. This is Eve's first day here and she has a twisted ankle."

"It's okay, Mom. I'm gonna stay here until it's time to go to bed. Then Vittorio can help me. After all, what are good-looking cousins for?" Eve's eyes twinkled in merriment at the new turn of events. She'd obviously never seen her mother bested, and this proved too good an opportunity to pass up.

"Eight o'clock?" David asked again, but Suzanne knew it was a demand.

She had no choice. "Eight o'clock."

He smiled again, but this time it reminded her of a hunter spotting his prey. "Great. See you then." He gave Eve a different smile, a far more indulgent one. "Nice to meet you, Eve. I hope I get to know you better."

"Oh, I'll be right here! Besides, I'd love to hear more about what Mom was like when she was my age. It seems that it's a taboo subject around our place."

"Remind me to tell you," David answered, then headed toward the breakers on the other side of the promontory.

He had no idea how much of a threat those words were. Both relief and fear of exposure filled Suzanne once more. Perhaps she needed to think of another way out of this dilemma. Perhaps she needed to find a way to get the girls to end their trip a little early, so they could all head back home.

"What's going on?" Eve asked as David walked onto the stone pier and disappeared around a rock. "That gorgeous hunk was somebody you met as a teenager and you didn't snag him? How come? Did he have zits and no shoulders then? If that was the case, he sure grew a nice set of them over the years—shoulders, not zits, I mean. He's fantastic! Now I see why you were so preoccupied when you were in Florence! Wait until Dawn hears this. And she told me I was probably wrong!"

"Eve..." Suzanne had to stop her daughter's monologue. "There is nothing to tell, and there was nothing odd in my behavior in Florence. I was just eager to begin my novel, that's all."

Eve's gaze told her she didn't buy that for a minute. "Okay, Mom. So how long has he been here?"

"And I don't want to answer any more questions about David. He's none of your business."

"Didn't you just say that anything Dad did that affected the family was our business?"

"It's not the same, Eve. I am not affecting the family. I'm not even involved with David. And if I was, it would still be none of your business, because I'm not marrying again."

"But—"

"There are no buts." Suzanne spoke firmly. "So enjoy the sun and the sea and your cousins. But don't, under any conditions, interrogate David."

A heavy sigh escaped her daughter's lips. Giving her a light kiss on the top of her auburn head, Suzanne walked toward their apartment, Eve's suitcase in her hand. It reminded her of the first day she'd arrived and run into David. She'd felt drained and exhausted then, too.

She had to get through this without Eve and David getting together. To help her, she'd enlist Tina's presence whenever she wasn't around.

Vernazza

John got married and the children were hurt because they weren't invited to the ceremony. I hope he realizes that someday when its convenient for him to be a father it may be too late.

No one realized that I might be relieved. Now he has someone else to focus on. I hope it works for him be-

cause we both need peace in our lives. I hope he treats Connie well because she seems like a nice girl.

Eve is infatuated with David—I can see it in her eyes. She told him that she and her sister had different fathers. I shudder to think of what might happen if David found out the truth.

10

"YOUR DAUGHTER is as beautiful and, from the twinkle in her eye, twice as precocious as you were at her age." David's voice came to her on a wave of heat, engulfing her in hell. Everything he said brought another wave. Her state was either born of fear, or she was having hot flashes. She'd bet on the first.

"Is your other daughter like her?" David asked.

Then she knew. Her skin wasn't hot and clammy from hot flashes. It was stark terror, pure and simple. "Yes."

"Aren't we talkative tonight," David teased. "Apparently you're not grasping the concept of conversation. I ask a question, you answer. Then you ask a question and I answer. It's a simple process, but a necessary one if two people are going to converse."

She swallowed hard, trying to relieve the dryness in her throat. "Really? What a revelation."

David leaned back in his seat and stared across the table at her. He seemed to be able to tune out the noisy revelers at the other dinner tables as well as a party of drinkers across the piazza.

"What's the matter, Annie? Am I boring you?"

"It's not that. I'm just tired. That's all."

"Tired from what? Your daughter's only been here a day."

Suzanne had had all the pressure she could take. That thought led to anger, which gave her something new to focus on. It felt good.

She threw down her napkin on the table. "Now listen up. I am not in the habit of telling outsiders my problems. I choose what I want to talk about. So when you badger me into talking now, you're actually making sure that we won't speak again in the future."

David watched her as she spoke. His gaze remained fixed, his expression void of emotion. "Why are you so leery of talking about your family?"

Her anger flared into a full-fledged forest fire. "None of your damn business."

"Is it because your marriage might not be all you've pretended it is?"

"None of your damn business." She almost spat the words through gritted teeth. "I'm leaving you now," she said, her anger now very audible. "And I would appreciate it if I never saw you again. Please have a pleasant trip home and *leave me alone!*"

She stood and brushed by him, squeezed through the close-set tables and headed toward her apartment. Eve's laughter tinkled on the evening breeze as she talked to her cousins and some other teenage tourists several tables away. Vittorio would help her up the apartment stairs later. Right now, Suzanne needed her own privacy, and having Eve around to ask more probing questions wouldn't be conducive to lowering her blood pressure.

She didn't halt until she was in her bedroom and once more at her window, staring at the dark alley below. Then the tears began to run.

She'd done what she'd promised herself she'd do. She'd broken up with David sooner than she wanted to, but she'd done it. She should feel good about ending this relationship before her daughters were hurt by her secret.

So why was she so miserable?

"Because I still love him," she sniffled. She'd loved him when she was eighteen and, God help her, she still loved him. It no longer mattered that he'd walked off and let her suffer the consequences of their actions. It didn't matter that she had ruined her own chance of happiness, that a life without him lacked the effervescence that made the days sparkle.

She'd known it then and knew it now. But there was nothing she could do about it.

Eve and Dawn were hers. She'd borne and raised them, taking pride in every accomplishment and comforting them through every downfall. She loved them more than she loved life itself. They were a part of her that no one, nothing could replace.

But that doesn't take away from your love for David! that annoying voice shouted. It was true. There were a thousand kinds of love, and she felt a different kind for each of the people in her life. She would always treasure her daughters—as she would David.

When one treasure threatened the other, what was she supposed to do?

The answer was the same. "Dammit!" She punched the wall, scraping her knuckles on the thick stucco.

It served her right. Her own impetuous actions had gotten her in this spot. She'd thought she'd learned her lesson, but she hadn't. Twenty-two years later, she was repeating that mistake.

FRUSTRATED, David stared up at Annie's window. Years ago she'd been stubborn, wonderful and impetuous. She was still all those things, only this time she was hiding something. He didn't know why, but he knew something was wrong.

Eve's laughter drew his attention. She could have easily been her mother when he'd first met her. And her lively and impetuous spirit was so much like her mother's, too.

What had happened to make his Annie change so much? Was she so disappointed with what life had offered that it had crushed her spirit?

The only thing he could imagine was that she felt bad about cheating on her husband. Well, it wasn't the first time a woman had done so, and he wasn't the first man to have taken a married woman to bed. But he didn't feel good about it, either.

He was also smart enough to know that no man or woman could be coerced into cheating on a good marriage. But from everything he'd seen and heard, David would swear that Annie's marriage had been shaky even before he came on the scene. David was sure she'd picked a fight tonight so she wouldn't have to explain it.

That was it. It had to be.

Taking a deep breath, he promised to use all the patience he had and allow her some space while she mulled over the problem and came to the same conclusion that he had. Then they could begin making plans for the rest of their life.

David tried to reassure himself that that was all that stood between the woman he loved and himself. But somewhere deep inside, where it could twist his gut into a wrung-out mess, was the knowledge that he was kidding himself. Something else was wrong, and it wasn't going to be easy to fix.

But there hadn't been a solution twenty-two years ago, and there might not be one this time.

SUZANNE WAS EXHAUSTED from keeping Eve company. Her daughter kept questioning her about David and their past, clearly thinking it romantic that two people should meet years later and both tragically wounded by love—Suzanne a divorcée, David a widower. Eve obviously believed that fate wanted Suzanne and David together. Eve's youth and naïveté made for a difficult day. And after her restless night, she was both mentally and physically exhausted.

Late that afternoon, Vittorio gallantly carried Eve downstairs to sit on the smooth black rocks in the sun. Eve probably could have negotiated the stairs in grand style, since she'd given up the pretense of a hurt ankle, but she was plainly enjoying Vittorio's attentions.

Suzanne heaved a sigh of relief for the wonderful quiet, but rejoiced too soon. Not fifteen minutes into her solitude, someone knocked on the door.

"You look like hell." It was David.

She ignored the concern in his voice and the soft look in his blue eyes. All it would take was a little caring, and she would crumble to the floor in a burst of self-pitying tears.

"Didn't we decide to call it quits?"

"No," he corrected softly. "*You* did. I wasn't asked."

"The results are the same."

"Hardly," he told her dryly. "You agreed and I didn't. That doesn't sound like a joint decision to me."

"It doesn't have to be a joint decision!" she retorted. "This isn't a partnership, David. One of us has decided to call off our... our relationship. The results are the same. Our time together is over."

David walked to the middle of the room, then turned toward her, hands on his lean hips. "Let me get this straight. You've decided that our relationship is over, and I have no say in the matter except to say goodbye. Is that right?"

Her heart felt as if it were being torn in two, but there weren't any choices left. David was her dream, but the reality of David in her life would be a nightmare. "That's right."

His hands clamped on her shoulders, his fingers imprisoning the frail bones. "That's wrong." He bit out the words. "Relationships are between two people. So are the decisions that make that relationship continue or dissolve."

"You're hurting me," she said softly, feeling the pressure of his fingertips more than actual hurt.

"I'm sorry, Annie." He uttered a deep sigh and closed his eyes. When he stared back down at her, they were a deep, indigo blue. "But you hurt me, too, and I don't understand why. I know you care. You show it in a million different ways."

"Of course I care," Suzanne said, trying hard not to cry. "But it's not enough. Nothing is enough to justify continuing with this." She wondered whom she was trying to convince: David or herself?

"Is it because you're still married?" His voice was soft. Understanding. "Because if it is, believe me, your marriage isn't worth salvaging. If it were, you wouldn't be here for the summer. You wouldn't be with me at all."

Suzanne began to protest, but David stopped her. "Annie, I know you. It's been obvious from the beginning that your marriage was over, if not in deed, then in thought. You couldn't make love to one man if you were involved with another. It's just not in you."

How did he know her better than she knew herself? It wasn't right. His knowledge of her felt like a breach of privacy. The thought was enough for her to gather her anger around her like a cloak of righteousness. "You have no idea what's in me and what's not! And because I don't happen to care for this relationship as much as you do, you will *never* know me well enough to make that judgment."

David's expression hardened to granite. "You don't mean that."

She felt her chin wobble, and gritted her teeth. "Yes, I do."

"Then your little *fling* is over and you're ready to go back to that dreary existence you call a marriage?"

She refused to think of the lonely life she'd left behind, the one that was waiting for her return. "Yes."

He stared deep into her eyes as if searching for the truth. When he seemed to find what he was looking for, he turned and walked through the door, leaving her inside the lonely apartment, reminding her how empty her existence would be without him.

She listened to the hollow sound of his footsteps echoing down the stairs, then the slam of the door. He was gone. For good.

Suzanne sat down on the couch and stared out the window. There weren't enough tears in the world to shed for him, so she shed none. Instead, she just sat quietly and felt her heart shrivel.

Eve came up much later and didn't notice until the following morning that her mother had changed. "Mom?" Eve asked in a hesitant voice. "Are you okay?"

Suzanne tried a smile, but it felt stiff and formal. "I'm fine. Just tired."

Eve buttered her fresh-baked bread and continued to chat. "Well, Vittorio filled me in on Mr. David Marshall last night. He tells me that you two have been together every minute." She paused to take a bite, then attacked. "So how long has this been going on?"

Suzanne stood and began picking up the used dishes. She couldn't look at her daughter. She could hardly talk about David without crying. "It's over. There's nothing to tell."

"What do you mean? I heard that... Mom? What's wrong?"

"Nothing's the matter, honey. But this is my problem, not yours."

"Did he hurt you? Did that snake in the grass take advantage of you?"

No matter how much her heart hurt from losing David, she couldn't help but laugh at her daughter's choice of phrases. High school was a breeding ground of trite sayings, but the kids had never heard them before, so they thought they were new. "David is a very nice man who has a family he's returning to. It was very nice to see him again and reminisce about our lost youth. Please don't read any more into it than that."

"Do you love him, Mom?" Eve asked softly, apparently unwilling to let the subject go. "Is that it?"

Eve's sympathetic voice was Suzanne's downfall. Tears formed in her eyes. She blinked twice. "I won't discuss it, Eve," she told her, throwing the words over her shoulder before running the stairs to the bedrooms above. She needed time to get herself together, and that couldn't be done in a minute. Especially not in front of her daughter.

DAVID SLAMMED the last of his shirts into his bag, threw a shaving kit on top and gave the zipper an angry closing twist. He did everything automatically, for his thoughts were consumed by Annie, the woman who had been in his dreams for years—but who in real life had turned him down.

He loved her. He loved her so deeply he could die of the pain of knowing the rest of his life would be a void because she wasn't with him. But he wouldn't. From experience he knew he'd go on. He'd do all the things he was supposed to do, say all the right words, even smile and laugh on cue. But that wasn't really living. It was no better than marking time.

He ought to know. Although he wouldn't have changed his marriage because of Jason he had marked time for twenty-two years. He'd done such a good job, he'd gotten used to a marriage of contentment rather than one of deep and abiding love. Until he'd met Annie again. He'd searched her out, found her, and fallen in love with her all over again. Not just the kind of love a young boy feels; now there was the deep need of a man's love. The kind of love that made him wonder how he could have existed all this time without it. Without her.

But Annie didn't feel the same way. In fact, he'd bet she hardly felt anything. She'd only wanted an affair, while he'd been stupid enough to hope their relationship was forever.

Stupid! The word rang in his head, pounding out its own rhythm. He'd been stupid to waste his dreams, believing in a figment of his overactive imagination.

He picked up his leather suitcase and slung the long strap over his shoulder. Well, it was time for him to begin living a life of his own. He deserved that much.

Jason had called last night. On the spur of the moment, David had told him to stay where he was in Milan and he'd meet him there for a weekend. Jason had sounded relieved, and David had a feeling that his son was lonely for family. It was exciting to be in Europe on your own, but it was also a little frightening.

He and Annie needed time away from each other to work out their emotions. When he returned in three days, Annie might be a little more receptive to talking over their differences.

And if Annie still wouldn't allow him to be in her life, then he'd forget her. Then he'd start playing the role of the merry widower. Moving with determination he shut and locked the door, then slipped the key into the mail slot.

He looked neither to left nor to right as he strode across the courtyard toward the train station. Only when a young girl stepped into his path, stopped and placed slim hands upon an even slimmer set of hips did he see it was Eve, fire in her eyes, who was trying to glare him into attention.

Despite his bad mood, he found his mouth quirking into a smile. He could have been a fire-breathing, fifty-foot-high dragon, and he had the feeling she'd still have come after him.

He paused. "I gather you have something you have to say?"

"I certainly do." Eve's eyes blazed. "I just want to say that after what Vittorio told me about you and my mom, and then the way you've treated her, I think you're a pretty immature man."

David raised his brows. "Since I'm not sure what Vittorio said and I don't know what you're referring to, I can't defend myself against your charges."

"Vittorio said you two have been together ever since Mom arrived."

"Right."

"And Mom's been hurt, I can tell. Since no one else has done that, I'd say it was your fault."

"Aren't you hanging me without benefit of trial, judge or facts?"

She looked surprised for a moment, then shook her head. "No. Mom's miserable and you're the culprit. I just want you to know that I hope you never have a chance to do this to anyone else. If I thought it would work, I'd cast a spell to make sure you couldn't do this again."

David tried not to grin. "If I remember correctly, at our first meeting, you thought I was good for your Mom."

"I was wrong."

"Couldn't you be wrong now?"

"Mom wouldn't be hurt if you were nice."

"No." David's next thought was grim. "But your Dad might."

"Since they're divorced, I don't think so. Besides, I gave up any hope of reconciliation long ago, and now that Dad's remarried, it's impossible."

"Remarried?" he questioned cautiously.

Again Eve nodded. "So, that wasn't what hurt Mom. You did."

David's thought swirled. They had been divorced long enough for her ex-husband to marry? Damn her! "How do you and your sister feel about that?" he asked, stalling for time.

"We weren't worried until now," Eve answered angrily. "Dawn's new job and my first year at college mean that Mom's going to be alone. And in a depression, thanks to you."

Alarm bells rang. "Whatever I'm supposed to have done, I plead innocent."

Eve ignored his defense. "Now Mom will have to handle everything by herself and it will be harder than ever since we're not going to be there to help her."

"Shouldn't Dawn still be in college?"

"She already finished. She's beginning her new job in Baton Rouge." He saw the vulnerability in her eyes, and cursed himself for goading her.

"Sorry, Eve. But whatever the reason for your mother's depression, I'm sure it has nothing to do with me. She wouldn't allow me to get that close."

Eve stood straighter. "Well, I just want you to stay away from my mother. She doesn't need some Johnny-come-lately messing up her life. She deserves much better."

Eve turned sharply and walked toward Vittorio, who stood just outside the restaurant kitchen, exasperation apparent on his thin face.

David adjusted the strap on his suitcase. With one last look at the empty window of Annie's apartment, he continued toward the train station.

This time anger spurred his steps. Annie had lied to him all along. He had never made love to a married woman—nor did he deserve the guilt that had eaten away at him for the past two weeks. The very guilt he'd made excuses for had never really been an issue.

Damn her!

He'd see his son, let his temper cool off, then return to have it out with her.

"You'll see me again, Annie," he promised aloud as he stepped onto the train and it pulled away from the station. "And this time we'll have that discussion I thought you were too distraught to have."

It was a promise both to her and himself.

Vernazza

David couldn't see me, but I watched him walk toward the train station. Even though he wasn't supposed to go for another day or two, he decided to leave. And I can't blame him. But my heart feels as if it's being torn out of my chest. I know I told him to go way yesterday, but he was still across the courtyard then. It wasn't as final, as devastating. As real. What will it be like to wake up in the morning and know that he's not in my life anymore? How can I wake up in the morning without being in his arms, without making love with him?

I was wrong to think that life was horrible when I was young and eighteen and without David. It's worse now, and he doesn't even know how bad that time was!

Time will heal. Everyone says so. Every song in the world repeats it.

I wish I was old. Then maybe this pain would be nothing more than a sad memory. Maybe I wouldn't care anymore.

But I doubt it.

11

SUZANNE knew she would never forget the next hours as long as she lived.

David had been gone only an hour when Eve crashed into the room, her eyes blazing with accusation and anger. "It's true, isn't it? David Marshall is Dawn's father, isn't he?" She didn't wait for an answer as she began to pace up and down. "I don't know why I couldn't see it! Even the way they smile is the same! My God! How could I have been so blind!" She twirled around, clearly looking for something to kick or punch in her frustration, then halted. "Why, Mom? Why didn't you tell me?"

Suzanne looked at her daughter with unseeing eyes. She didn't have to see. Her heart told her that she was either going to die, which would be a blessing, or she was going to lose that which she had nurtured, cared for and loved all these years—her daughters. She closed her eyes. When she opened them again, Eve was still in front of her, staring down as if seeing her mother for the first time and not really knowing her at all. She was a stranger to her own daughter.

There was no sense in denying David's place in her life. It would only make matters worse. If she'd thought she had paid for her mistake twenty-two years ago, she'd been wrong. The final payment was still outstanding. "How did you find out?"

"I confronted him downstairs as he was leaving. When he just smiled and went on his way, Vittorio came down hard on me. He said it was your business if you wanted to keep in touch with *Dawn's father*, that you were the only one who could make the decision about your relationship with him, and I had no right to interfere."

"I see," Suzanne said tiredly. Somewhere deep inside a small spot of relief grew; after all this time the secret was out. But that spot was so small, she couldn't even focus on it. Right now she had a problem on her shoulders that felt as big as the world.

Eve slumped down beside her and stared out the window. "I know you've got a good reason for not telling us. I know it."

"Of course."

"And I know that Dawn wants to know, too."

Suzanne knew better than to try to admonish Eve to keep it secret. It wasn't right for the two sisters not to be able to communicate completely. And even if it were, Eve still couldn't keep a thing to herself.

"I'll go to Florence immediately," Suzanne told her.

Eve didn't look up. "You don't have to. I called Dawn and she's on her way. She'll be here in about four hours."

Suzanne's heart thumped so hard it hurt. She took a deep breath to ease the pain. "You already told her?"

"I didn't mean to. But I did."

"Oh, Eve," Suzanne whispered, feeling even sorrier for her daughter than she did for herself. "How did she take it?"

"She was furious." Suzanne saw Eve's bottom lip tremble. Slowly she turned to her mother, showing the tears that cascaded down her cheeks. "I'm sorry, Mom. I'm so sorry."

"I know, honey. It's all right."

"Does this mean Dawn isn't my sister anymore?"

"No. Dawn is still your sister. I'm still your mom, your dad is still your dad."

"I wish he'd never come here." Eve's expression was as vulnerable as a small child's. "I wish I'd never pretended to have a bad ankle. I would never have met him. Things would still be the same."

Then, as if she were five years old again, Eve burrowed her head in Suzanne's breast and cried because her world had crumbled. It had. Suzanne cradled her close, rocking her with a tuneless lullaby. Her tears also flowed unchecked, streaming down her cheeks to plop onto her daughter's dark locks.

The next few hours of waiting were so painful that by the time Dawn entered the apartment, the only emotion Suzanne could register besides her grief was relief. Soon it would all be over; then she would know what the future held for her daughters and herself.

Dawn stood belligerently in the doorway, boots, jeans and bulky cotton sweater accentuating her lithe form. She dropped her backpack to the floor with a heavy clunk.

"Is it true?"

"Sit down, Dawn. Let's discuss this," Suzanne suggested wearily.

"I don't want to sit down! I want an answer."

Suzanne felt the panic radiating from her daughter. Part of that emotion was her own, too. She took a deep breath and tried for control. "I'll tell you all about it when you sit down."

Jerky movements propelled her daughter into the straight-backed chair by the window. "Tell me," she demanded, her voice as tight as her look.

The moment Suzanne had dreaded all her life was finally here. It was twice as hard as she'd thought it would be, three times harder on all their nerves.

"It all began twenty-two years ago, when I came to visit Tina," she began, and slowly told them the story. She didn't try to defend her actions of those days. She couldn't even gloss over them. Instead, Suzanne told the truth as best she could, explaining only the parts that pertained to Dawn.

When she was through, Dawn was still rigid with anger, hands clenched on her thighs. "Why didn't you tell me before this?"

Suzanne rubbed her forehead, wishing the head-ache away. "I wouldn't have told you at all if I could've helped it, honey. If Eve hadn't found out, we wouldn't be having this conversation."

Dawn's eyes grew large in accusation. "You would have kept this a secret forever, wouldn't you?"

"Yes."

Dawn's face crumpled and Suzanne moved toward her.

"No!" Dawn held her hand out like a traffic cop. "I don't want your comfort! All my life you told me a lie. *All my life!* Don't you know how often I wished my real father was alive—that I could meet him? I could have! Why didn't you tell me the truth?"

Once again tears streamed down Suzanne's cheeks, but she refused to give in to the grief-inspired sob-bing that welled in her breast. She deserved this dia-tribe, and deep down inside had prepared for it ever since she began the charade. "I love you, Dawn. I didn't want anything to hurt you. Ever."

"And what about Dad?" Dawn asked, jumping up and pacing the room. "How does he feel about this? Did he know my real father was alive? Did he think of me as being someone else's daughter all this time? And what did my...biological father say when he found out about me?"

Eve sat quietly next to her mother, her body filled with such tension that Suzanne thought she would break from it.

Taking her younger daughter's hand, she covered it in a gesture of commiseration as she answered Dawn's question.

"Your dad always knew, honey. We met when I was a freshman in college. He took both of us under his wing."

Dawn's eyes were closed as she listened. But her hands rubbed up and down her jean-clad thighs in agitation. Her anger was still apparent in her every move. "Who decided to lie, Mom? You or him?"

Suzanne shrugged, still refusing to allow the tears to fall. "It just happened."

"And it ruined my life forever. Once this gets out, my friends can all say 'poor pitiful Dawn—her mother had an affair and then misplaced the man! Isn't it wonderful that another man came along to help hide her mistake.'"

"Hardly, honey," Suzanne replied. "Your life would have been hell if I had kept you and not married, instead of bringing you up in a traditional atmosphere. Look around you. You're in Europe as a college graduation gift. I wouldn't call that ruin."

Dawn strode to her backpack and picked it up from the floor. "I'm going back to Florence."

"Dawn," Suzanne began, rising from the couch to stop her, then realizing that Dawn was probably doing the right thing. "Dawn," she said more quietly, gaining her attention.

Dawn halted, finally meeting her mother's gaze. Suzanne saw hurt and confusion in the depths of those blue eyes, emotions stronger than the anger she displayed. But the slight softening there also told Suzanne that she hadn't been cut out completely.

"Dawn, I love you. I'll understand any decision you make regarding our relationship, as long as you talk to me about it first. But I can't second-guess what's on your mind unless you tell me, so I want you to remember one thing. These aren't your teen years anymore. This isn't an argument between us—it's the past that's shedding a different light on our future. Please, for both our sakes, remember that I was younger than you are now when all this happened. By the time I was your age, I was a mother of two."

"That doesn't make your decision right. Eve, you can meet me at the hotel we stayed at in Florence if you want to," Dawn added, just before the door slammed in punctuation.

SUZANNE LEANED BACK and stared at the plane seat in front of her. Six hours ago she had caught a plane in Milan and was heading home. It was the end of her vacation. It was the end of everything. It didn't matter that her heart was breaking. It didn't matter that Dawn and Eve were in Pisa, both trying to work their way through the emotional destruction her lie had left behind.

She closed her eyes and tried to eliminate the look she'd seen on Eve's face as she tried to talk her mother out of leaving so early.

"But, Mom," Eve had cried. "You wanted this time to write. Why not do it here?"

"Because I'd rather be home right now."

"It's because of that man, isn't it?"

"No." Suzanne's voice had been firm. She'd had to maintain control of that conversation before Eve took the ball and ran with it to the wrong goal line. "And you can drop that train of thought right now. I'm going home because there are too many reasons here not to write."

So now Suzanne was on her way and no one would know her heart was breaking. It was her secret.

"Would you like a glass of champagne to celebrate your return?" the stewardess asked with her practised charm.

Unbidden, tears filled Suzanne's eyes. She swiped at them and tried to return the smile. "I'd love one," she said.

So much for pretence. The rest of her life was going to be lonely, because she knew now what she was missing.

The champagne was flat.

DAVID SAT ON THE TRAIN and tried to doze. His body swayed in unison to the clickety-clack of the wheels. He'd spent the day in Nice with his son, only to realize that he hadn't paid enough attention to the conversation he'd had with Eve; he'd been too wrapped up in Suzanne's response. It wasn't until the next day that he figured out what it was. Eve had said her sister had graduated from college. That would make her on the far side of twenty-one. That information created an entirely different picture from the one Suzanne had wanted him to see.

His heartbeat seemed to stop. His skin broke out in a cold sweat. Ideas flew through his mind. No matter how much he denied it, the facts spoke for themselves.

It was possible that Dawn was his child.

His child!

Although he loved Annie with everything in him, he didn't let that love blind him to her. She was stubborn, reserved, occasionally angry and opinionated. Only she'd learned how to hold her tongue. It was an attribute David wasn't sure he admired. Her spark and fire and enthusiasm were a few of the things he'd respected, longed for. But those qualities were gone. Now she was far more reserved, the fire extinguished by life's lessons and some dark secret he hadn't known ... until now.

Now he was inundated by facts. Fact one: Annie was no longer married. Fact two: Annie had tried to get ahold of him when they were young. She'd said so. And it would have had to be out of desperation. Fact three: she had two daughters, and one of them was old enough to be his. That meant one of two things. Either she'd had an affair straight from his arms, which was what she clearly wanted him to think, or he was the father.

His gut clenched. Thanks to his friend Jerry, she hadn't known how to contact him.

No wonder she'd been so shocked to see him! He was the devil from the past, bringing back all kinds of anguishing memories.

He frowned. So why hadn't she accused him of being a no-good coward, a seducer of innocents? He would have. If he'd been in her place, he'd have done everything possible to cut the offender out of his life.

Another memory hit him. *Dawn looks like her father, while Eve looks like me,* Annie had said. That meant Dawn looked like him!

The train wasn't moving fast enough. Given the level of adrenaline pumping through his system, he could have gotten off and run next to it. It would be another hour before he reached Vernazza. And Suzanne.

Then he would have the answers to the questions he should have raised to begin with.

Somewhere over the Atlantic

I think I've missed some of the best things in life and there's no way to go back and claim them. Regret engulfs me. Eve has called for the last two nights to tell me that Dawn loves me and it will work out. It's nice to hear my eighteen-year-old try to console me, but what does she know about the human spirit? Right now, Eve is trying to believe that everything has a happy ending. I believe Eve's wrong about Dawn's anger easing toward me, but I can't be sure either one of us is right.

Someday, if we're very careful, we'll rebuild our relationship because Dawn will realize just how much I love her. Maybe.

It's funny, but when the truth finally came out, I felt relieved. For one brief moment, I thought there was a chance David and I could be together. But it didn't last long. Dawn wouldn't be that forgiving. If I saw David again it would end my relationship with her. She hasn't been forgiving in the past, I can't see any reason for her to change now. She hasn't forgiven John and me for our deception. Having David in my life would rend us beyond repair. Hell, for all I know, it's beyond repair now.

It's nine o'clock at night in Vernazza. I can picture Tina and the kids clearing up the restaurant kitchen. Arturo walks by Tina and brushes a kiss on her cheek. Occasionally he pats her behind. She laughs and scolds him. He looks unrepentant.

I wanted that kind of relationship so badly, and I never had it. And now John is married and sharing his life with someone else. I'm jealous. No, not because

*of John's marriage, but because I have no one to share
with. Will I always feel this alone?*

HE'D HIT some all-time lows before, but David had
never felt so alone. He sat on the piazza's low stone
wall by the fishermen's church and stared out to sea.
He'd only been gone three days, but everything had
changed. Suzanne's apartment was empty. She'd
taken her clothing and gone. She'd either run away
from him or decided that she couldn't stay here any
longer. And he needed to know which it was.

He'd tried to find Tina, but suddenly her children
couldn't speak English very well, and he wasn't sure
which apartment she lived in. Since he'd returned, she
hadn't come downstairs at all.

For lack of anything else to do and with a deep desire to be near Annie any way he could, David pushed
off the wall and strode toward her now-empty apartment. He opened the unlocked door to the dining area
and stepped inside, closing it behind him. For reasons he couldn't fathom, it felt as if Annie was still
here. Any minute she'd be coming out of the kitchen
and into his arms. Any time now....

Desolation washed over him as he realized just how
much he wanted her to be here. *Needed* her to be here.

Her perfume still scented the air. It mingled with
memories, filling his mind with pictures and thoughts
that hurt as much as they helped.

Suddenly none of the problems, the deceit, the misunderstandings were as important as seeing Annie and being with her again.

Looking back on his life, he'd always been lonely, had always thought that if he was good and honest and caring, he would be rewarded. And his reward would be to find Annie, marry her and live happily ever after. Being a dreamer, he'd never gone beyond the dream to a few of the practical points involved in seeking his reward. He knew how to go about finding her. And, although he hadn't said it yet, he knew what he wanted to say. He was a lawyer; he should be able to plead his own case!

Whom was he kidding? He never won against Annie's convoluted logic. He couldn't cut through the words she threw out as a decoy to find the root of the problem. Especially in the past two weeks. When she'd returned from Florence, he'd noted a change in her—and nothing he'd done had helped him find out what caused it.

A thousand questions and no answers.

His hands balled into fists. "Dammit, Annie. Come back to me!"

He forced himself to take deep breaths and release the tension that held his body almost in a death grip. Glancing around, he caught sight of a picture frame that had been pushed toward the back of the buffet, facedown on the polished wood. He recalled having seen it before, and to distract himself decided that he might as well satisfy his curiosity.

It wasn't until he finished fiddling with the back stand that he sat back and looked down at the photo it contained. It was a photographer's studio picture. The background was a mottled blue, outlining the girls' dark hair and peaches and cream complexions. Both had long dark hair, both wore angora sweaters: Eve's was blue and her sister's a kelly green. Eve looked more subdued than usual. Dawn looked as if subdued was a word often used to describe her. Even her smile was shy. But shy didn't mean that this young woman was a wallflower. She was beautiful. Judging by the tilt of her chin, she was also stubborn. And the glint in her blue eyes said she was determined to achieve her goal—whatever it might be. But it was her features as a whole that made his hands shake, the familiar angle of her head as she shyly stared into the camera that tightened his gut.

David could have been looking at his son's twin. Jason had the same-shaped face, the same shy but determined eyes, the same full lips that tilted slightly more on one side than on the other. Even their slim, youthful necks were structured the same way.

He was looking at his daughter.

Now he could see why Annie had been so reticent, could understand why she'd been so frightened and withdrawn.

And that understanding brought more questions. Did Dawn know about him? Would she want to meet him? Or did she hate him for leaving her mother to fend for herself?

He closed his eyes and felt the pain Suzanne must have felt when she realized she was carrying his child. And that pain intensified because he'd been cheated out of a lifetime with his daughter.

Someone had stolen those precious moments from him and he couldn't seek retribution. *He* was the thief. Because he'd never gotten in touch with Annie, he'd spent the last twenty-two years dreaming of her, while she must have spent that same time cursing him.

One question overrode all others. Now what?

SUZANNE HAD BEEN HOME for a month. She woke up every morning and began the same routine. The early morning sun was still hot and bright, pretending summer hadn't ended. She stared out her kitchen bay window, enjoying the lush tropical garden just outside. It had been peaceful . . . then.

Dawn lived in Baton Rouge now, sharing an apartment with another girl and working for a major accountant's firm. She loved her work, enjoying the challenge of living independently, away from home, and working at a career she loved.

Things had been touchy at first, but slowly Dawn and Suzanne had reformed a wobbly relationship. When they first returned, Dawn hadn't spoken for a while. But her curiosity had finally gotten the better of her, and she'd slowly begun asking questions about her father, his son and his marriage. Suzanne had answered the best she could with her limited knowledge, glad that she could contribute anything that might keep Dawn talking to her.

Neither had discussed getting in touch with David. With New Orleans an hour and a half from Dawn's door to her mother's, she had begun to take advantage of that and visited often under the pretense of picking up something she needed from her bedroom. Each short visit made things easier between them.

Eve was in her first year of college and living in a dorm outside Shreveport in upper Louisiana. Suzanne was tickled by the phone calls from her younger daughter—she was never sure if Eve was going to play the grown-up or the child. It varied. She was growing up so quickly, and Suzanne was so proud of them both.

Everything was settled and in place and she should have been feeling on top of the world. Instead, ever since she'd returned home from Vernazza last month, she'd been unable to gather the energy to be content. No matter what she saw, what she felt, how she heard things, it all reminded her of David.

Tears welled into her eyes. "Let's face it, Annie," she murmured, calling herself by David's pet name by way of doing penance. "You might as well get used to this kind of life, because this is what it's going to be like from now on."

From now on. She'd spent a little less than twenty years in a marriage, then chosen to end it. Now she would spend the rest of her life alone—all because she was in love with the wrong man. She constantly reminded herself that seeing him could harm her relationship with her children. Especially her. Making the right choice had never been easy, but it was *right*. She had to remember that.

It didn't matter that the future stretched in front of her like a vast abyss. Her choice was made.

Tears felt like salve to her bruised soul. Hands covering her face, Suzanne cried until the hurt grew temporarily numb. Then she dried her eyes and got back to the business at hand. Sitting down at the computer, she lost herself in the story she was telling.

She was amazed when the doorbell rang and she glanced at the clock three hours later. It was hard to believe time had disappeared so quickly.

Looking tired but as sexy and handsome as ever, David stood with one shoulder propped against the doorjamb. He stared at her as if he would either shake her or kiss her, she wasn't sure which. At this point it didn't matter.

She smiled tentatively, but let her eyes feast on every feature, every sexy line. It was like Christmas again.

"You haven't moved away or hidden yourself in another city." His voice was low, deep and its tone slightly reserved. But she heard a small note of relief.

She swallowed hard. "No."

His blue eyes narrowed. "That's amazing. I would have expected you to flee to the ends of the earth before you'd confront me with the truth." The air of surprise became a hard, accusatory tone.

Her heartbeat quickened. He didn't know the truth. He couldn't know. She was just panicking, reading her own fears into his visit here. Tina had sworn that she and her family had not said a word to him about Dawn. "What truth are we discussing?"

His lips thinned. "You know what I'm talking about. The truth that made you run away from Vernazza—and me."

She crossed her arms over her breasts. She would bluff this out. "Which was?"

For a moment he looked startled. "You mean there are more lies than the ones I know about?"

Her eyes widened. "I don't know about any lies, but I'm willing to humor you until you explain what you're talking about."

David stared down at her for a long, uncomfortable moment. "I'm talking about the fact that you and I have a daughter, and once we met again you never bothered to explain to me the what, how and why of it. In fact, you never discussed it at all."

She straightened her shoulders and stared him in the eye. "I don't know what you mean and I don't care if

I ever see you again." Her hand clutched the door-knob. "Goodbye."

She tried to close the door in his face. With even quicker reflexes, David placed his foot in the door, preventing her.

"This is the showdown, Annie. And you won't be able to run from the problem this time. Instead, we're going to face it, talk about it and work it through."

Panic set her words free and accusation threw the words at him. "Did you meet Dawn? Talk to her? Tell her?"

David shook his head. "No. I roared like a lion at Tina's family, trying to get answers on where you went and how I could get hold of you. But I never saw Dawn—only a photo you left behind. But I want to. That's why I want both of us to face this problem, instead of running away from it."

"Run from the problem?" she repeated, aware that her voice sounded even harsher than his had been earlier. She laughed, but knew it was hollow. "You must have a very short memory, David. You walked away from me and never returned, never contacted me, never even sent a postcard to let me know whether you lived or died."

Hands on hips, she glared at him. "And when I think of what I went through, I have no sympathy for you at all. You have no daughter! *I* do! I know, because I remember the past twenty-one years very well!"

She walked toward him, stepping onto the porch. David took a step back to allow her room. Her finger pointed at his chest, making an indentation on his knit shirt. "*You* decided to be noble and not call at all! *You* never gave a thought to the eighteen-year-old girl you'd sworn love to while you were still engaged to another! *You* were the one who conveniently forgot to give me your address."

David opened his mouth, but her finger moved from his chest to his lips, effectively silencing him as she continued her tirade. After all, she'd waited twenty-two years to say some of this. Now that the secret was out she might as well get the rest out of her system. Her anger was so strong she almost swore she smelled brimstone, and it fueled even more rage.

"You decided to play God, and everyone else had to fend for themselves! That wasn't your right, but you did it anyway. Meanwhile, *I* had to raise our child by myself. *I* had to confront my parents by myself. *I* had to decide what to do every day of her life." By finally releasing the words, she also released the tension that had been building inside her all summer. "Not you, David," she said more softly, closing her eyes at the pain of those thoughts. "Me."

"Oh, Annie," he whispered hoarsely. And when she looked up, tears were streaming down his face, too.

Her hand shaking with wonder, she reached up and wiped away a tear. "You're crying."

"So are you."

"I know," she said tiredly. "I have a right to cry. You don't." Her words were strong, but the anger was gone, washed away by the flood of anguish in her soul.

"I lost the right to cry when I left you. Everything I did after that was based on my own decision, my own life, my own circumstances." His hands clamped on her shoulders. "But you've got to believe me when I said I never thought about making babies and leaving you stranded. It never occurred to me—youthful ignorance, I suppose. I believed Jerry when he said he'd given you my address and telephone number."

Such intense pain glimmered in his eyes that Suzanne had to turn away for a moment. She swallowed hard.

David's grip on her shoulders tightened. "I thought I was the only one in our relationship who had suffered. I believed you were blithely strolling through your life while I was chained to my responsibilities. There wasn't a day that went by that I didn't taunt myself with the thought of you having a wonderful, happy time, while I was trying to work two jobs, raise a son and care for my wife."

For the first time they both seemed to realize they were discussing something too personal to talk about outside, where the whole world could hear them.

Suzanne turned and retreated into the coolness of the entryway. David followed, slipping his hands from her shoulders as she closed the door behind them.

"Annie." David's voice was filled with as much longing as Suzanne knew showed in her own eyes. However, instead of walking into his arms, she retreated to the living area. She would not succumb....

"Annie." This time his voice was stronger. More determined to gain her attention. "Barbara was my wife by law. And for the first couple of years we really tried to make that relationship work. But it didn't, because by nature she was my best friend. I *loved* you."

Suzanne's eyes blazed with tears and frustration. "You made love to her."

He nodded, his gaze solemn. "I don't deny it and I won't apologize for it. You made love to your husband. But that didn't mean you didn't care for me. We both convinced ourselves that love was the reason we were together. That doesn't diminish our partners or us. It just was."

She shook her head from side to side, more to dispel the web he was weaving around her heart than to deny his statement. "I don't care what happened in the past anymore. Don't you see? It doesn't matter! Dawn is all that matters. She found out the truth, and it almost killed our relationship. She's my daughter, and I almost lost her."

"She'll adjust," David stated confidently. "When we meet and I get a chance to talk to her, she'll understand. Wait and see."

She shook her head. "No. As long as you—or what you say—could hurt her, nothing will ever change. I will not allow anything or anyone to hurt Dawn."

"You're not giving me a chance."

"About the same chance you gave us."

"That's bitter."

"That's truth." All her stiffness left. "No, that's not the truth, David, but it's as close as I can come to allowing you into our lives. Dawn is *mine*. And I will *not* lose my relationship with her for anyone. Not even you."

"Let me talk to her. I want her to understand. I want to be a part of her life, too."

For a split second Suzanne remembered the look on Dawn's face when they'd confronted each other in Vernazza. So much anguish and hurt. Too much for a young woman to manage at once. "She has a father who's already a part of her life, David. She doesn't need another."

He stood with hands on his hips and smiled down at her. "You're not married anymore, are you?"

Suzanne couldn't meet his eyes. "It doesn't matter whether I am or not. The fact remains that you're leaving here and not returning. Ever."

He reached out and rubbed the backs of her arms, his fingers trailing up to stroke her neck. "You're asking me to leave the one thing I've waited for all my life. You want me to sacrifice my happiness forever? You want me to lose the woman I love? You ask me to not love you, not think about you, not crave you. It's just as impossible."

Her heart hurt at finally hearing the words. She'd waited all her life for those words, only to have them uttered in the wrong time and place. The wrong life.

"Damn you for not calling," she whispered, staring at him as if committing him to memory. She was.

"I already am damned."

The silence was impenetrable.

They both jumped when the doorbell rang and looked guiltily toward the door as it swung open—to admit Dawn. She stood in the entrance, wearing jeans and a mint-colored, oversize sweater.

"Mom," she called before turning to see him. "Hi," she said in a more subdued voice, her expression going from surprise to puzzlement. Then her quizzical air turned into something else—something Suzanne knew was recognition. Her eyes touched on David's hand resting on her mother's neck, then she looked away. "I just need something from my closet. Excuse me," she mumbled quickly. And darted up the stairs.

The heavy silence was almost tangible.

"She's so beautiful," David murmured hoarsely. Awe and regret filled his voice.

"Yes." It was all Suzanne could say. Dawn's presence was bringing them together in a way that no amount of talking would ever have done.

His hand dropped from her neck, leaving her skin chilled. "I love you, Annie."

"I know."

He opened his wallet and pulled out a card, placing it carefully on the bookcase behind her. "I can't make you change your mind about us, Annie. You have to do that by yourself."

"I won't." She shook her head and swallowed, already reliving their past and trying not to look at their bleak future.

His warm breath caressed her as he leaned forward and brushed a kiss onto her forehead. "I know."

His steps echoed hollowly through her soul as he walked across the wooden floor and out of the room. Out of her life.

12

TWENTY MINUTES LATER, Suzanne was still numb. She sat at the kitchen table staring at the butcher-block top. A coffee cup sat on the table in front of her, its contents cold and bitter. Dawn's footsteps squeaked across the kitchen ceiling as she walked from closet to bed and back again. She hadn't recognized David, after all. Everything was the same as it had been before. No damage had been done.

That thought should have been a comfort. It wasn't.

When Dawn's sneakered footsteps trod lightly on the stairs, Suzanne tried to paint a smile upon her lips, but her heavy heart wouldn't let her. Instead, she stared at her daughter as she walked into the kitchen.

Dawn was the feminine image of her father. The fact that Suzanne had raised her to be the dynamic woman she was showing promise of becoming was an added bonus.

Dawn walked straight to the coffeepot and poured a cupful. Holding the warm mug in both her hands, she stared out the kitchen window, her back toward Suzanne. "Mom? Who was that man?

"Is he the guy from Vernazza that Eve talked about?"

What a funny way to refer to the man who'd fathered her! But Suzanne understood. Dawn was putting distance between herself and the man she didn't know. "Yes."

Slowly Dawn turned around. She held the cup of coffee in front of her, but the liquid hadn't been touched. Steam drifted lazily before her solemn expression. "He really is my father, isn't he?"

Suzanne's heart thumped so heavily, she thought her ribs would crack. "John is your father, honey. He raised you."

Dawn continued to stare at her mother, her gaze steady. "David Marshall is my biological father, isn't he?"

Swallowing hard, Suzanne couldn't find her voice. She nodded her head and waited for her to erupt. Dawn's anger in Vernazza was still vivid in her mind.

"Eve was right, I look like him." Dawn sipped at her coffee, made a face and reached for the creamer.

Suzanne's fingers clenched in a death grip as she waited. Nothing happened. Nothing was said. No one shouted. Dawn reached for a spoon and clanged it loudly in the cup as she stirred. The high-pitched sound grated on Suzanne's already taut nerves. Still she bit her lip and waited.

Finally Dawn spoke again. "If I had stayed downstairs, would you have introduced us?"

Suzanne nodded. "I wouldn't have had much of a choice."

"Would you have told me who he really was?"

"I wouldn't have to. You already knew the name, Dawn. You'd have recognized it." Her voice was a mere croak by now.

"Did he know who I was?"

Suzanne cleared her throat. There was an inevitability to this scene. It was a release, like having a bad dream disturb your sleep over and over and finally knowing that this would be the last nightmare. Everything else would be real. "Yes."

Dawn nodded her understanding. She walked to the kitchen table and took the seat across from Suzanne. "Do you think he wants to meet me?"

"Very much so." Suzanne reached across the table and gave Dawn's hand a squeeze. "But he won't push it either, Dawn. He's as scared of being rejected by you as much as I felt guilty about the circumstances surrounding your birth. Morals were very tight and everyone seemed so judgmental in those days."

"Why didn't you give me up?" Dawn asked.

"I had your grandmother's support in making my own decision, plus their word that they would help me financially and emotionally. I couldn't have done it without them." Suzanne stared down at the hands covering her daughter's. She'd been three years younger than Dawn when she'd made that decision. "Being pregnant with you, thinking about you made it so that when you were born I couldn't imagine life without you."

Dawn looked repentant. "I've been rotten about this whole thing, haven't I?"

"I think I understand that, honey," Suzanne said gently, realizing that she did now understand some of Dawn's problems. "Sometimes getting angry is another way to cover up our own overwhelming feelings of confusion. You didn't know what to think and needed time to adjust."

"Can you tell me about it now?" Dawn asked shyly. And with relief Suzanne complied, finally giving her more details of her birth and early years—something they had not managed to discuss before. While she spoke, Dawn stared at her as if trying to absorb her mother's life. Suzanne forged ahead, now finding the words where none had been present before.

When she was through, Dawn looked down at her cup of cloudy coffee. "What really happened to David Marshall? Was he just playing the field?"

"No. He went home because his best friend, the girl he was engaged to marry, was crippled in an auto accident. Instead of telling her about me, he married her."

Suzanne saw Dawn's eyes dart to her—eyes that so reminded her of David. A stab of pain hit her heart. "Do you believe he really did that?" her daughter inquired.

Suzanne nodded. "He's an honest and honorable man, honey. Someone you'd be proud to know. It's one of the things I loved about him. We were just too young to realize the consequences of our actions."

The young woman's eyes widened as another thought appeared to occur to her. "You were Eve's age! Good grief, I can't imagine Eve having a baby and trying to raise it!"

"I know." Suzanne grinned. "Except it happened to me, honey. And because it did, I did the only thing I knew to do. I married your dad."

Dawn pulled her hands away, putting them into her lap. "And told me my real dad was dead."

Suzanne was surprised that the bitterness that had been there a month ago was now gone. "Because for me he really was." She wanted to reach out and clasp her daughter's hands. She wanted to explain how much soul-searching had gone into that decision. Instead she apologized. "I'm so sorry."

"I knew all along it was a lie."

Now it was Suzanne's turn to be surprised. "You did?"

Dawn nodded, her face solemn.

"How?"

She shrugged. "I don't know, I just did. Then, when I was about seven or eight years old, I was going through Grandma's photo albums and ran across some pictures of you with him in Vernazza. When I showed them to Grandma, she said it was my father. I stole the picture and have kept it in my drawer all this time." She glanced down at the tabletop.

"Why didn't you talk to me about this then?"

"Because any time my father was mentioned, it was as if you didn't want to say his name in case Dad overheard you. I thought it might be too painful for you."

"It was, but not for the reasons you believed." Suzanne's voice clouded with emotion. "You should have talked to me, honey. We could have aired the problem and never gone through all this."

Dawn looked up and for the first time Suzanne saw her daughter's tears. "What should I have said? 'Gee, Mom, I'm sorry love didn't work out for you the second time'?" She gave her mother a watery smile. "I wasn't supposed to know about the first time."

Suzanne tried to smile back, but couldn't. "I didn't want a lie between us, but I also didn't want you to know any of this."

Dawn looked as if she understood. "I wasn't really hurt, you know. Mostly I was curious. But when I realized that my real father was still alive and that others had met him, talked to him, even liked him, I got scared. It was something I didn't want to cope with! My own personal fairy tale was suddenly real. I didn't want that. A real father would say no, tell me the dream boat I brought home was a nightmare, would have gotten angry with me when I did something silly. My imaginary father couldn't do that."

"Even though you'd always dreamed of him, he was a threat?"

Dawn nodded. "When I found out you two were together again, I panicked. What if he not only didn't like me, but liked you better?"

"And so you ran to Florence," Suzanne said softly.

Dawn nodded. "For a while I couldn't talk about it without crying. I couldn't ask the questions I wanted to ask and get answers I couldn't cope with. I was still scared."

Suzanne felt Dawn's hurt and wished she could take her into her arms, kiss her and make it better, just as she had when Dawn was a child. "And now?"

Dawn chuckled but it sounded forced. "Lately, anticipation of hearing the story from you was half the fun."

"Well, I wish I'd known how you felt. I would have battled it out with you this summer, instead of doing everything in my power to keep you from knowing about him." Suzanne knew her voice was shaky.

"And obviously to keep the two of us apart," Dawn added, hitting the nerve of the problem. Suzanne had been hiding things from Dawn much as she'd hidden her old relationship with David. She hadn't wanted to tell her story. Now the story was told. It hadn't been half as painful as she'd thought it would be.

"He wants to meet you so badly. He says you look a lot like his son, Jason, and that you're beautiful. But I think he's scared a little, too."

"Good," Dawn said with visible relief. "I'd hate for us to be the only two worrying about it. That would be awful!"

But Suzanne couldn't yet put the situation to rest. "Are you shocked or angry?" She tried to read her daughter's expression but couldn't. "Talk to me. Please."

Dawn's smile was shaky, but her gaze was clear. "I love you, Mom, you know that. I'll always regret that you didn't tell me sooner. But a part of me is excited at finally having the puzzle pieces fit together. I'm still a little scared about getting to know him and even more about that first meeting. But I'm ready. I've waited for this day for a long time."

Instead of condemnation, her daughter was offering her reprieve. Then came the thought: there was nothing to stop her from being with David except herself. She felt a smile form on her lips at the thought. Bubbles began forming inside, making her buoyant.

She leaned forward and took her daughter's hands into her own. "Dawn, how would you feel if, after all these years, your father and I got together?"

"I don't know." Dawn tilted her head, her usually clear forehead creased in a thoughtful frown. "I think it'd be odd, but I'd love to spend some time with him and get to know him myself." Her brows rose. "And I have a half-brother?"

Suzanne grinned as she nodded. "He looks a lot like you. I saw his picture. Jason is Eve's age."

If Dawn had looked surprised before, she was shocked by that piece of news. "Really?"

Suzanne nodded, giving her daughter's hands another light squeeze. "Are you going to be all right?"

Dawn smiled broadly. "I'm fine, Mom. Just to know that my real father's not a three-headed monster helps. But the relief of knowing that he's nice and not a real . . . jerk, helps even more." Her expression grew very serious. "What are you going to do now? Go after him?"

Suzanne stood and walked around the table. She leaned against it and cupped her daughter's solemn face in her hands, staring deep into the unflinching blue eyes. "I love you, honey."

"I know. I love you, too."

Suzanne tucked a stray strand of dark hair behind her daughter's ear, using it as an excuse to touch her. "No one could ever take your place in my heart, honey."

"I guess you're telling the truth. We made it through my rocky youth and we're still talking."

"And we'll talk more, whether David Marshall is in my life, your life, or both our lives."

"Mom," Dawn hesitated, but Suzanne saw the tears that shimmered in her daughter's eyes.

"I know, honey," she said, her own words forced out in spite of the lump in her throat.

They wrapped arms around each other, their hug telling of emotions too deep to surface readily into words. Yet. Suzanne was sure God had touched her heart. She was so lucky to have her family, to have a relationship that warmed them all.

"Aren't you going to tell him?" Dawn's question brought her back to the present.

Suzanne laughed, then kissed the tip of her daughter's nose. "Yes, I am. Right this minute. All I have to do is figure out where he went."

"Well, his car was a rental," Dawn said, giving the name of the rental company.

"Thanks, see you later," Suzanne told her, reaching for her purse as she went out the back door. "Get back to work!"

Dawn laughed. "I was wondering when you'd notice!"

Suzanne started her car and slipped out of the opened garage, then revved the engine and raced toward the airport. Praying David hadn't left consumed her thoughts. Fifteen minutes later, she pulled up to the rent-a-car lobby and jumped from the automobile.

David stood at the counter, talking to a young woman whose smile attested to her interest in the handsome man in front of her.

Suzanne stood stock-still, watching him, absorbing his every movement. When he turned to leave, she called his name. "David?"

HE TOOK IN her flushed face, her wide eyes, her warm, uptilted smile. The lavender sweater stroked and hugged her breasts the way he had wanted to. Then he remembered. "Yes?" He kept his tone distant, using the voice he reserved for secretaries and salesmen he didn't know. He wasn't about to allow his feelings to come to the fore again and get stomped on. He couldn't handle that.

"I love you." Her voice was soothing, soft. Honey sweet. Her words brought back painfully sweet memories. She had said the same thing in Vernazza all those years ago. He swallowed hard to forget this summer, when she'd said those words again. Instead of forgetting, his memory provided him with an instant, Technicolor replay. They had just made love and her mouth had been soft and wet with his kisses, her gaze languid, sexy, replete. He'd been filled to overflowing with her love.

He stared at her, hoping the memory would go away. "Don't," he finally managed to say.

"Dawn knows you came to visit."

He felt as if he'd been poleaxed. "What did she say?"

"That she wants to meet you. That she recognized you from a picture she ran across years ago. That she's interested in meeting her brother."

"I couldn't blame her if she was hurt and angry."

Suzanne laughed. "Neither could I, but she isn't. She's a little excited and a lot scared." Suzanne shook her head in wonder. "Just like her mother is right now."

"Her mother has a right to be," he said in a low tone, remembering the lies she'd told him. Especially the one about being married. Every time he'd made love to her he'd felt guilty. Not guilty enough to stop, but guilty enough. "Now what happens?"

She looked confused. "Don't you understand? I love you!"

He was afraid to believe that she meant any more by saying those words now than she had this summer. "According to you, you've always loved me. But you lied to me then, too." He fixed her with a narrow-eyed gaze, pinning her to the middle of the lobby floor. "So what's different?"

She raised her head and tilted her chin. "No more lies. No more fear." But her bottom lip wobbled, giving her away. "I just thought you'd want to know."

"You're letting me go?" he asked.

"I can't keep you here."

"Are you sending me away?"

"Only if you don't want to stay."

Exasperation filled him. He took another step toward her. "Are you going to continue to lie to get your way?"

She looked like a little girl caught in her first lie. Repentant but relieved. "No."

"Are you going to tediously explain all the past to me so I know what's been going on in Dawn's life and in yours?"

"Yes."

"Are we getting married?"

Suddenly the solemn expression left her eyes, to be replaced by the mischievousness he hadn't seen in twenty-two years. "Only if you're very, very good."

He wrapped his arms around her waist and pulled her to him. "Oh, honey," he said softly with a growl deep in his throat. "I'll be so very good, you'll never want anyone else."

Craving the taste of her, he claimed her lips with his.

Along with the thunder pounding through his veins, another thunder surrounded them. When they looked up, at least ten people were applauding. The two girls behind the counter were wiping away tears. One man in a long overcoat blew his nose. Mother and daughter look-alikes sat on a nearby bench and clapped.

David grinned. Still holding Annie at his side, he nodded to their audience, accepting their accolades. "I told you I was good," he said softly.

"You're so good, you're bad. And that's just the way I'll always want you."

"We'll make a million more memories before we're old, Annie. I promise. Beginning right now." He took her hand in his and walked her out the door. "Where's your car?"

"Right here," she said breathlessly, pointing.

David held out his hand for the keys. He helped her in, then shut the door, as if his touch would insure that she wouldn't escape while he walked around the vehicle. Once inside, he had to take her into his arms one more time.

"When we're seventy years old, we'll probably still be necking in cars." After his kiss, she rested her cheek against his chest and breathed in the scent of him. It was heaven.

"When I'm too old to drive, I'll put one up on blocks in our garage," he promised.

Annie laughed and the sound flooded the car, washing his body with a soothing sound. It felt as if he'd been given back his youth.

"I can't imagine you being too old."

"If I'm too old, you will be, too."

"Never." Her answer was prompt. "I may be too wrinkled, too senile or too fat. But I'll never be too old for necking with you."

He never got around to putting the car into gear. He had to hold her in his arms just once more before he drove. "Neither will I, darling. Not as long as you're with me."

Their kiss sealed that promise and so many others still unspoken. And it was just the beginning.

Oklahoma City, Oklahoma

We've been married almost a year, and I didn't know it was possible to love David more than I did when we exchanged our vows. But I do. Although we live in Oklahoma now, the girls aren't really that far away and visit often. And when they're not here, I'm talking to them on the phone.

The kids have all adjusted slowly but well. Jason had the hardest time. Raised as an only child, he's not quite sure what to do with two young women who claim him as brother. But our first Christmas together was terrific. The first day everyone walked on eggs, being so polite I thought I'd tear my hair out. David was the patient one. He invited our neighbor Joan and her husband Marv to play Boggle. It started out a little stilted, but by the end of the game, all the kids were shouting and laughing at each other. It was the merriest Christmas ever.

And the best thing of all is that Dawn has blossomed into such a vivid and outgoing young woman around David and me. She discusses things I never dreamed we'd be talking about. And she especially enjoys asking David about the things we said and did when we first met. In her own way, Dawn has a romantic streak as big as Eve's. I love watching them together and seeing the bond they're creating.

But I love being alone with David, too. We take walks, go bike riding, grocery shopping or just sit in front of the TV and he holds me. I never knew how much I craved to be held and stroked until he showed me what it was like.

I give thanks every day. I'm so thankful to God for showing me what happiness is. I was worried that He hadn't heard my prayers, but I guess He did. In fact, I think He knew that until I learned a few lessons, I wasn't going to appreciate what He was getting ready to send my way.

Well, I did and I do.

I'll say it every night before I go to sleep, and every morning when I wake up next to him. Thank you, God.

PENNY JORDAN

Sins and infidelities . . .
Dreams and obsessions . . .
Shattering secrets
unfold in . . .

THE HIDDEN YEARS

SAGE — stunning, sensual and vibrant, she spent a lifetime distancing herself from a past too painful to confront . . . the mother who seemed to hold her at bay, the father who resented her and the heartache of unfulfilled love. To the world, Sage was independent and invulnerable— but it was a mask she cultivated to hide a desperation she herself couldn't quite understand . . . until an unforeseen turn of events drew her into the discovery of the hidden years, finally allowing Sage to open her heart to a passion denied for so long.

The Hidden Years—a compelling novel of truth and passion that will unlock the heart and soul of every woman.

AVAILABLE IN OCTOBER!
Watch for your opportunity to complete your Penny Jordan set. POWER PLAY and SILVER will also be available in October.

Take 4 bestselling love stories FREE

Plus get a FREE surprise gift!

Special Limited-time Offer

Mail to
Harlequin Reader Service®
3010 Walden Avenue
P.O. Box 1867
Buffalo, N.Y. 14269-1867

YES! Please send me 4 free Harlequin Temptation® novels and my free surprise gift. Then send me 4 brand-new novels every month, which I will receive months before they appear in bookstores. Bill me at the low price of $2.64 each—a savings of 31¢ apiece off cover prices. There are no shipping, handling or other hidden costs. I understand that accepting the books and gift places me under no obligation ever to buy any books. I can always return a shipment and cancel at any time. Even if I never buy another book from Harlequin, the 4 free books and the surprise gift are mine to keep forever.

142 BPA AC9N

Name	(PLEASE PRINT)	
Address		Apt. No.
City	State	Zip

This offer is limited to one order per household and not valid to present Harlequin Temptation® subscribers. Terms and prices are subject to change. Sales tax applicable in N.Y.

HARLEQUIN®
OFFICIAL SWEEPSTAKES RULES

NO PURCHASE NECESSARY

1. To enter, complete an Official Entry Form or 3" × 5" index card by hand-printing, in plain block letters, your complete name, address, phone number and age, and mailing it to: Harlequin Fashion A Whole New You Sweepstakes, P.O. Box 9056, Buffalo, NY 14269-9056.

   No responsibility is assumed for lost, late or misdirected mail. Entries must be sent separately with first class postage affixed, and be received no later than December 31, 1991 for eligibility.

2. Winners will be selected by D.L. Blair, Inc., an independent judging organization whose decisions are final, in random drawings to be held on January 30, 1992 in Blair, NE at 10:00 a.m. from among all eligible entries received.

3. The prizes to be awarded and their approximate retail values are as follows: Grand Prize — A brand-new Mercury Sable LS plus a trip for two (2) to Paris, including round-trip air transportation, six (6) nights hotel accommodation, a $1,400 meal/spending money stipend and $2,000 cash toward a new fashion wardrobe (approximate value: $28,000) or $15,000 cash; two (2) Second Prizes — A trip to Paris, including round-trip air transportation, six (6) nights hotel accommodation, a $1,400 meal/spending money stipend and $2,000 cash toward a new fashion wardrobe (approximate value: $11,000) or $5,000 cash; three (3) Third Prizes — $2,000 cash toward a new fashion wardrobe. All prizes are valued in U.S. currency. Travel award air transportation is from the commercial airport nearest winner's home. Travel is subject to space and accommodation availability, and must be completed by June 30, 1993. Sweepstakes offer is open to residents of the U.S. and Canada who are 21 years of age or older as of December 31, 1991, except residents of Puerto Rico, employees and immediate family members of Torstar Corp., its affiliates, subsidiaries, and all agencies, entities and persons connected with the use, marketing, or conduct of this sweepstakes. All federal, state, provincial, municipal and local laws apply. Offer void wherever prohibited by law. Taxes and/or duties, applicable registration and licensing fees, are the sole responsibility of the winners. Any litigation within the province of Quebec respecting the conduct and awarding of a prize may be submitted to the Régie des loteries et courses du Québec. All prizes will be awarded; winners will be notified by mail. No substitution of prizes is permitted.

4. Potential winners must sign and return any required Affidavit of Eligibility/Release of Liability within 30 days of notification. In the event of noncompliance within this time period, the prize may be awarded to an alternate winner. Any prize or prize notification returned as undeliverable may result in the awarding of that prize to an alternate winner. By acceptance of their prize, winners consent to use of their names, photographs or their likenesses for purposes of advertising, trade and promotion on behalf of Torstar Corp. without further compensation. Canadian winners must correctly answer a time-limited arithmetical question in order to be awarded a prize.

5. For a list of winners (available after 3/31/92), send a separate stamped, self-addressed envelope to: Harlequin Fashion A Whole New You Sweepstakes, P.O. Box 4694, Blair, NE 68009.

PREMIUM OFFER TERMS

To receive your gift, complete the Offer Certificate according to directions. Be certain to enclose the required number of "Fashion A Whole New You" proofs of product purchase (which are found on the last page of every specially marked "Fashion A Whole New You" Harlequin or Silhouette romance novel). Requests must be received no later than December 31, 1991. Limit: four (4) gifts per name, family, group, organization or address. Items depicted are for illustrative purposes only and may not be exactly as shown. Please allow 6 to 8 weeks for receipt of order. Offer good while quantities of gifts last. In the event an ordered gift is no longer available, you will receive a free, previously unpublished Harlequin or Silhouette book for every proof of purchase you have submitted with your request, plus a refund of the postage and handling charge you have included. Offer good in the U.S. and Canada only.

HQFW·SWPR

HARLEQUIN® OFFICIAL SWEEPSTAKES ENTRY FORM

4-FWHTS-2

Complete and return this Entry Form immediately – the more entries you submit, the better your chances of winning!

- Entries must be received by **December 31, 1991**.
- A Random draw will take place on **January 30, 1992**.
- No purchase necessary.

Yes, I want to win a FASHION A WHOLE NEW YOU Classic and Romantic prize from Harlequin:

Name _____ Telephone _____ Age _____

Address _____

City _____ State _____ Zip _____

Return Entries to: **Harlequin FASHION A WHOLE NEW YOU,**
P.O. Box 9056, Buffalo, NY 14269-9056   © 1991 Harlequin Enterprises Limited

PREMIUM OFFER

To receive your free gift, send us the required number of proofs-of-purchase from any specially marked FASHION A WHOLE NEW YOU Harlequin or Silhouette Book with the Offer Certificate properly completed, plus a check or money order (do not send cash) to cover postage and handling payable to Harlequin FASHION A WHOLE NEW YOU Offer. We will send you the specified gift.

OFFER CERTIFICATE

Item	A. ROMANTIC COLLECTOR'S DOLL (Suggested Retail Price $60.00)	B. CLASSIC PICTURE FRAME (Suggested Retail Price $25.00)
# of proofs-of-purchase	18	12
Postage and Handling	$3.50	$2.95
Check one	☐	☐

Name _____

Address _____

City _____ State _____ Zip _____

Mail this certificate, designated number of proofs-of-purchase and check or money order for postage and handling to: **Harlequin FASHION A WHOLE NEW YOU Gift Offer, P.O. Box 9057, Buffalo, NY 14269-9057.** Requests must be received by December 31, 1991.

ONE PROOF-OF-PURCHASE

4-FWHTP-2

To collect your fabulous free gift you must include the necessary number of proofs-of-purchase with a properly completed Offer Certificate

© 1991 Harlequin Enterprises Limited

See previous page for details.